The Bat Mitzvah Club
Debbie's Story

by Shayna Meiseles

The Bat Mitzvah Club
Debbie's Story

edited by Leah Lax

created by Esther Frimerman

Merkos L'Inyonei Chinuch
770 Eastern Parkway
Brooklyn, New York 11213

Copyright ©2001 by
Merkos L'Inyonei Chinuch
770 Eastern Parkway
Brooklyn, New York 11213
(718) 774-4000
FAX (718) 774-2718

Order Department:
291 Kingston Avenue
Brooklyn, New York 11213
(718) 778-0226

www.kehotonline.com

ISBN 0-8266-0029-8

Manufactured in the United States of America

To my mother.

E.F.

CHAPTER ONE

I just can't stand it. Nothing's the same anymore. I can't even eat dinner in my own home like a normal person. Just thinking about her family meals lately made Debbie scowl. *Why do our meals have to be "family meeting time?" They want me to talk about "things" and I just don't have anything to say! And they seem to have plenty to say. Sometimes I wish my parents would just send me to my room if they don't like something.*

Debbie thought about her father's first words at dinner the night before. "You're eleven now, and not a little girl any more... and it's almost time for your Bat Mitzvah."

Bat Mitzvah?!? How can I even think about a Bat Mitzvah at a time like this? I don't have time to study for it! Math is hard enough, and the first big swim-meet of the season is tomorrow, and my swim time's still off. Even if I had the time, Miri would interrupt me every five minutes. She's such a pest! Why does she always have to get into my things?

Well, here she was, called to another "family meeting" at dinner. Debbie sighed. She had to admit to herself, the very idea of a Bat Mitzvah frightened her. She wanted to wail, *I have no time! I have no room!*

Debbie thought about that morning before school. She had just finished her breakfast and she was gathering her books to leave for school, when her mother turned to her in the kitchen.

"Debbie," she said, "make some time for us to talk tonight. We have got to make plans for your Bat Mitzvah."

"Uh, Mom...I'm gonna be late today. I've got a study date with Leah. I might even eat dinner over there."

"Debbie..."

Debbie looked at her watch. "Oh, no. It's almost eight o'clock." Quickly she took her books, grabbed her lunch, and kissed her mother. "Bye, Mom!" And off she ran, with her mother standing behind her with her mouth open. Debbie felt a lttile guilty as she walked to school. She knew she was avoiding the subject, but she couldn't help it. It wasn't that she wanted to irritate her mother. But she kept wishing that the Bat Mitzvah would just go away.

And now Debbie was sitting down to dinner with her parents and Miri after all. It seemed they had waited for her so they would be able to eat together. Debbie saw the look on her parents' faces and inwardly rolled her eyes.

She sat down and ate most of her meal in silence.

I wouldn't mind talking with my parents. But not because I'm supposed to, like a school assignment. This was the first time she remembered feeling self-conscious with them.

Debbie's mother passed her the salad bowl. "Debbie, let's talk about that Bat Mitzvah, okay?"

Debbie pointed to the salad. "Did you hear about all those poisons they spray lettuce with?" Her mother sighed. "All right, Debbie. I understand," she said. Debbie reached for her glass of orange juice and her hand knocked it over. An orange puddle spread across the table. Debbie watched the juice spill over the edge of the table and to the floor for a moment before she jumped up to wipe up the mess. She felt strange, as if some other girl had knocked over that glass. *I know that wasn't really an accident. I kind of meant to do it. Why did I do that?*

"Honestly, Debbie," her father said as he backed away from the dripping table. "You seem so jumpy."

As Debbie went to the kitchen for some paper towels, her father's words burned in her ears: *Jumpy? I do feel jumpy sometimes. Like a rabbit.*

Debbie came back to find her father had moved the dishes and started to clean up. They worked together, but her father's kind face had a frown on it. "Are you getting enough sleep? Maybe we should make your bedtime the same as Miri's."

Miri giggled.

Very funny. "She's only nine," Debbie protested.

"And you're almost twelve," her father countered. "When a Bat Mitzvah is coming, it's time to get at least a little serious."

That's the way it goes. Every night. No getting out of it. This Bat Mitzvah stuff is getting harder and harder to ignore.

Debbie wanted to get up early the next morning so she could meet Leah before school, but she was up late studying math and overslept. Again. She ate her breakfast quickly and did not speak to anyone. Before her parents had a chance to begin last night's topic where it left off, Debbie pushed away from the table.

Debbie's mother glanced at the clock and looked startled. "Where are you running off to?" Debbie was gathering her books.

Mrs. Solomon looked at her daughter's long, willowy limbs that seemed to be stretching longer by the day now, her firm mouth and wide-set deep brown eyes, and sighed. Debbie always seemed to be running headlong somewhere, and always with a determination about her that left her mother breathless. But Mrs. Solomon knew the sensitive, hesitant side to her daughter as well.

Debbie ran out the front door without answering. She stopped short when her mother called after her. "Debbie, you have to walk Miri to school today!" Debbie turned to see her mother standing on the front step, gesturing to Miri to come out of the house.

"But Mom, I'll be late."

Mrs. Solomon was expecting protest. "It's early yet. You have plenty of time."

"I have to meet Leah," Debbie called back. She stopped and turned.

"Both your father and I have early meetings on the other side of town—so we can't drive either of you. You'll just have to walk your sister. I'll call Leah and tell her why you can't make it."

"Okay, Mom," Debbie replied, but her voice did not sound like it was okay at all. Miri appeared on the step beside her mother.

Debbie glared at Miri. *How can she be so small for her age and such a big pest?* It seemed like Miri was making a show out of kissing her mother goodbye. Miri's features matched the rest of her—a small, thin nose, round, little mouth, expert at pouting, and lively blue eyes like her mother. She pertly tossed her light brown hair back and took forever to make sure her coat was buttoned up. Then she took an age, mincing delicately down the steps on her short, thin legs, then along the sidewalk to Debbie's side, carefully avoiding the cracks. *Look at her. Little Miss Innocent. Sometimes little sisters can be so annoying. Like right now.* Debbie scowled at her.

"Can't you be any slower about it?"

Miri shrugged and playfully pushed her fingers into her

hair, adjusting her hair ribbon. Then she tossed her head back as if to say: "What of it?"

Something was slowly dawning on Debbie. She looked down at Miri's wrists. "What's that under your sweater?" Debbie demanded, pulling on Miri's sleeve.

"N-nothing," Miri stammered, suddenly dropping her princess demeanor. "What are you talking about?" She struggled away.

"This!" cried Debbie, pulling out the cuff of her new white blouse from underneath Miri's sweater. Debbie was furious. "Miri, how dare you! And it doesn't even fit you. Look at how you had to fold up the cuff! Wait until I tell Mom. You're really going to get it."

"I don't see how you'll get a chance to tell her," Miri replied in her most annoying voice. "You'll be at your Bat Mitzvah Club."

"My what?" Debbie replied.

"Bat Mitzvah Club. Look inside your lunch bag."

Debbie opened up the bag and pulled out a piece of paper. There was the name, address and phone number of some organization. In the center of the leaflet, the notice read:

Welcome to the Bat Mitzvah Club!
Join us every Tuesday at 4:00 p.m.

There was a note at the bottom hurriedly scribbled in her mother's handwriting: "You're all signed up. Starts today!"

Debbie took a step backward. "But, but..." she stammered. Debbie looked up when she heard the honk of a car horn. She saw her petite mother looking up over the steering wheel, waving as she pulled away. An expensive silk flowered scarf was impeccably knotted at the neck of her new blue suit. Her lipstick shone. Her blue eyes and delicate features seemed to be from another place—Miri's inheritance and not Debbie's. For an instant, Debbie imagined herself behind the wheel, already taller than her mother, breezing easily down the boulevard away from the Bat Mitzvah Club meeting, leaving her mother behind. Debbie raised her hand distractedly, but did not wave. She was still thinking of the Bat Mitzvah Club notice. "But..." Then she turned again when she heard another car horn and saw her father's wave. "What about the swim meet?"

Debbie reluctantly walked Miri to the elementary school. Then she continued the few blocks to her own school, the Chicago Hebrew Academy. She could have saved herself some time by cutting across an empty lot and using the back route, but she did have a few extra minutes before school started and she wanted to delay her arrival a bit.

As she walked, she thought about what had just happened. *Bat Mitzvah Club?* She groaned. *It's not like I don't like birthday parties or presents or Jewish celebrations. I was looking forward to this year ever since I moved to the Hebrew Academy from public school, because it's a whole year of parties. It was so much fun this year. It seemed like all the girls in my class were celebrating our Bat*

Mitzvahs together! She paused. *But I didn't think about having to be at the center of my own Bat Mitzvah. If only one of the parties didn't have to be mine. Why do these things have to be such a big deal?*

Leah's brother David had had his Bar Mitzvah a couple of years ago. The whole affair was so fancy. Too fancy. She still shuddered when she thought about the gigantic salmon laying in the center of the buffet table. Its eyes were open and staring at her. *That thing looked alive.* The caterer used thin slices of cucumber to replace the fish's fins. *I don't know why that fish made me nervous.* The rest of the buffet table had platters of meats, sliced breads, salads, cakes, cookies and strudels. *Too much.*

Debbie had gone early to the banquet hall with Leah and Leah's mother, since Leah's mother wanted to check on the caterer and the last-minute arrangements. Debbie and Leah spent their time nibbling at the miniature cherry tarts—so many tarts in fact, that the waitresses had to shift over the rest of the pastries to fill up the empty spot. She embarrassed Debbie when she glared at them like that. But Leah didn't care.

Everyone made such a big deal out of David turning thirteen. Sure, he put on a prayer shawl and read from the Torah. Sure, he made a speech about becoming a man, but that made me laugh. I'm taller than he is. And, his voice cracks when he sings. She remembered how he led the service. After the ceremony, the rabbi congratulated David. Everyone cried a little and handed him checks as presents. Then the party started, and that was that. David seemed the same. He even looked the same. *Okay, maybe he's a little richer, but is he really suddenly a Jewish man?*

Now David's fifteen, and Leah and I are nearly twelve. And when I look back on his Bar Mitzvah, that's all I remember: the party with all those presents, that big salmon, and those tarts! Like a big show. That was the part that really made Debbie nervous—having to be the center of attention at a big show. *If that's what it is, what's all the money and time and hassle for—just to make me nervous?*

Debbie trudged along without really seeing where she was going. She remembered when her parents first told her that they were considering putting her into a Jewish school. She and Miri were already in their pajamas that summer night when they went downstairs to say good night. But instead of sending them back upstairs, her father asked them to sit down and talk. Debbie felt so grown up. She was only nine at the time. When Debbie went to bed that night, she lay awake a long time remembering her parents' voices. "You are a Jewish girl," she kept hearing. What confused her then was the way her parents acted like they had made a mistake. "We should have done this a long time ago," they said, "but we didn't know."

She felt lucky that she got to make the switch, but she still felt different from some of the other girls because of where she was coming from. Debbie liked the way there were other kids there that also came from public schools. Although she was now one of the best in her class in

Hebrew language, in the beginning she had to have a lot of tutoring to catch up. At least she knew several others at school who had gone through the same adjustment. In fact, there were kids at the school from all kinds of Jewish backgrounds. The changeover was easier for Miri, since she got to start a lot earlier. Still, at least now Debbie wasn't going through this Bat Mitzvah thing alone.

She almost bumped into someone on the sidewalk and she muttered an absent-minded, "Oh. Sorry."

Hmm... this Bat Mitzvah Club will either be interesting or a big waste of time. If only it didn't take me away from swim practice!

CHAPTER TWO

ight after math class that day and, wouldn't you know it, another surprise quiz, Debbie tried to meet up with Leah at her locker, but Leah wasn't there. *She ran out of math class so fast! She's probably rushing to the cafeteria line before it gets too long.* Debbie put her books away, grabbed her lunch bag, and hurried to the cafeteria. She wasn't especially hungry. Staying awake to study so she could pass her math test whittled her energy down to nothing. No sleep plus math test equals zero energy.

Debbie immediately recognized Leah's curly head of hair and her short frame from behind. Debbie was several inches taller. Leah's arm was raised in a gesture illustrating something to the person in front her, who was laughing. Debbie cut in behind her friend. Nobody minded that she cut in. Everyone knew she and Leah stuck to each other like glue. She turned and uttered her thanks to those behind her. Then she surprised her friend, still busy entertaining, with a tap on the shoulder from behind. Leah paused in mid-sentence, turned and smiled her familiar lopsided smile as she looked delightedly at Debbie with dancing hazel eyes. "Hi! What's up? Look at this! Dairy again. Nobody's pushing to the front of the line to get this food. Petrified cheese!" They were close enough to the front that a couple of the kitchen workers shot Leah a look, but the kids on the food line laughed.

Debbie waited quietly in the line, ignoring Leah's antics with her friend, selected a wobbly dessert, paid, and went with Leah to find a spot to sit.

The girls looked for their usual spot with their group of friends. "Hey, guys!" Sarah called, waving them over. "Eat with us. We'll all suffer together."

"You know, maybe we should do our science project on these sandwiches," Leah said, giggling. "We could figure out the absolute maximum amount of grease they could hold." Leah could find a way to make anything funny. All the girls wanted to be with her. Debbie was proud that Leah wanted to be her best friend.

"Looks like the cafeteria's already figured that out," Debbie said. The rest of the girls around the table laughed. Although she was quieter than Leah, Debbie had a quick and irresistible smile. She often came up with the punch lines for Leah's jokes. They were a team. Ever since they had met back in third grade, they'd been close friends. Once, when they were smaller, they tried to pass as sisters, except that no one would believe them. Debbie was taller and slimmer than Leah, and her hair was light brown and straight, like her sister (the only feature she seemed to share with Miri), while Leah's hair was dark and curly.

"What's going on, Deb?" Leah asked, turning toward her and twisting her dark curls into a barrette. "You seem a little spacey."

"Well," Debbie began, "you know how I've been struggling to get my time down in swimming."

"No rest for the perfect!" Jennifer teased, sitting across from her. Jennifer was also on the team, but she did not push herself the way Debbie did. Debbie envied that. *She actually enjoys swimming. And it never worries her.*

"I can't help it," Debbie said, pretending to whine, yet with a grin. "I just always feel I can do it just a little faster if I practice enough."

"Yeah," Leah replied, "and you will, too. You're not our best swimmer for nothing."

"Well, now I have a problem with practice," Debbie continued.

"Oh yeah? Me too," Leah said. "My parents are making me go to some Bat Mitzvah Club."

Debbie felt a wave of relief. "Me too!" she squealed. "I thought I was in this all by myself."

"Oh yeah?" Sarah said. "Don't forget, my Bat Mitzvah is before yours. My mother won't let me forget."

"So why don't you come to this Bat Mitzvah Club with us?" Debbie offered.

Leah jumped in. "You've still got me to sit right next to you, Debbie. We can pass notes to each other during all the boring parts."

Debbie looked at her curiously. *She sounds jealous! What's the deal?*

"Leah, are you jealous or what?"

"Well... no. Yes. Uh, maybe."

"I can have more than one friend." Debbie frowned at her. Leah didn't look as if she wanted to talk about it. Debbie purposely turned toward the other girls and away from Leah.

"This whole thing makes me so nervous," Debbie said. "You know what happens when the club sessions are over, don't you? It's not like there's just a test or anything. You just have to stand up in front of all the guests at your party and make a speech—and sound like you know something!"

"Oh, I'm not worried," Jennifer said. "I'll talk my Mom into writing mine for me. I'll just have to read it, and I'll make sure she keeps it short."

Leah glanced down at her arms. "Wow! Look! I'm getting goose bumps just thinking about doing a speech."

"Leah, you?! Yeah, sure," Debbie chortled. "Okay, let's say this Bat Mitzvah Club isn't a bad idea. At least the class will give us something to say for a speech. Still, what do we tell Mrs. Brown?"

"Coach Brown?" asked Leah. She looked startled, as if she could have possibly forgotten the name of their swimming coach.

"Yeah, Coach Brown," responded Debbie, too sweetly. "Not only do we have to miss part of practice, we have… "

"The swim meet!" Leah and Jennifer said together.

"I thought maybe you forgot," Debbie giggled.

"Me forget?" Leah said. "You won't let me forget. Okay, so we just tell Coach that you'll win your race no matter what."

"What!" Debbie exclaimed. "That means beating Rachel Levine!"

"That means beating Rachel Levine!" Leah echoed.

"But she's the champion!" Debbie said.

"She's the champ! Soon to be 'ex' if I know Debbie." Leah winked.

"Easy for you to say. You're not swimming against Rachel Levine. Don't make any promises I can't keep," Debbie replied.

"Yeah, right!" Sara said.

"Like I said, soon to be 'ex' if I know Debbie." Leah winked again.

CHAPTER THREE

The Bat Mitzvah Club met in one of the classrooms of a private school several blocks away. The school was old and did not have as many students as it had once had, so it often rented out unused rooms to various organizations. Debbie was familiar with the school because the Chicago Hebrew Academy often rented their auditorium for major affairs—like last year's school play. Debbie thought of the old brick facade of her school and their cramped classrooms. There was no auditorium. They used the lunchroom for assemblies.

In spite of her familiarity with the place, by the time Debbie and Leah found the right room, the Bat Mitzvah Club had already started. They could hear a woman speaking through the door. "Great start," Debbie whispered, as she pushed it open.

Debbie recognized a few girls from their class among

the group. There was Jennifer and Sarah, who waved at them. *So they did come!* Debbie smiled and nodded to them. But she did not know many of the faces. The two sneaked to the back of the room hoping to go unnoticed. Immediately, the teacher stopped and said, "Hello. I'm Mrs. Levy. What are your names?"

Leah stopped and looked at her. "We're Leah-and-Debbie," she said, as if they were Siamese twins.

Mrs. Levy smiled. "Who's Debbie and who's Leah?" she asked gently.

"Me, I mean, I am," Debbie whispered, sliding low into a seat.

"You're Debbie and Leah?" The class giggled. "Can I guess? You're... Debbie."

Debbie nodded, biting her lip. *I didn't even brush my hair since lunch time and its already four o'clock! Why didn't we come on time and just blend in?*

"So, I'll take another guess," the teacher said, smiling and turning towards Leah. "You're Leah."

All the girls laughed.

Nevertheless, for some reason she hadn't quite figured out yet, Debbie liked Mrs. Levy right away. Maybe it was the softness in her voice. Maybe it was that she was somewhere around her mother's age, and that she was wearing a blue suit with a flowered blouse, and blue was her mother's favorite color. *She seems smart, but not a showoff. Maybe she'll be nice.*

Mrs. Levy turned back to the class. "Well, I think you

are all going to be surprised. After this meeting, you girls are the teachers."

Debbie and Leah exchanged skeptical looks as if to say: "How could we be Bat Mitzvah teachers?" Debbie watched closely as Mrs. Levy walked around the room and gave each girl a shiny gold folder, a large red envelope, and a small clothbound book covered with flowers. When Debbie received hers, she fingered the cover of the flowered book and read the title: "Thoughts That Inspire Me." Debbie flipped open her book. All its pages were blank.

Mrs. Levy's eyes met Debbie's. "No, that's not a mistake," she laughed. To the whole class she explained, "The pages are supposed to be blank. This is for each one of you to write your own thoughts. What you write doesn't have to be directly about your Bat Mitzvah, although that's welcome. Write about things that happen in your life and how they make you feel. Write about how it feels to be eleven or twelve years old."

Mrs. Levy perched on the edge of her desk. She was of medium height, and neither heavy nor thin. Debbie did not feel she could pick her out in a crowd if she saw her from behind. All of the features of Mrs. Levy's face seemed slightly too big for her. Her eyes were large and heavy lidded. Her nose was… generous. Her mouth was full-lipped and wide for her face. The effect was not beautiful, but somehow sincere and appealing, as if to put emphasis on her words.

Mrs. Levy's voice grew wistful. She sounded almost like

she was a girl again. "I started writing in a journal when I was around your age. I wrote about how sometimes my parents or my brothers or my teachers were unfair to me. Other times I wrote about how everything felt great. Looking back now, I think the more I wrote about my feelings, the more I understood myself. Lots of times I got up from writing and felt that whatever happened to bring me down that day had lost all of its power over me." Mrs. Levy paused again, and looked up as if she'd almost forgotten where she was.

The girls were quiet and attentive. It seemed like Debbie could feel the flip-flop emotions of the young Mrs. Levy, and see them written on her expressive face. One girl shyly raised her hand.

"Do you still have your journal?" she asked. It was Sarah. Debbie caught her eye and smiled. Sarah smiled back. She pointed to her watch and then grinned and shook her finger at Debbie like a parent at a mischievous child. *What a tease. I hope I don't leave here late for swimming.*

"This will be our little secret. I do still have my journal," Mrs. Levy smiled. "I filled a few books. I kept it up for a few years after my Bat Mitzvah. They're packed away in a special, private place in my closet. Keeping them makes me feel like I'm holding onto the twelve-year-old part of me from a long time ago. What a special time of your life. It passes so quickly."

Mrs. Levy took a deep breath. She stood up. "What kind

of thoughts can you imagine other people in previous years have put in these journals? Go ahead. Let your imagination run wild."

Slowly, but steadily, more and more hands went up.

"Your problems," one girl said.

"Like what?" Mrs. Levy asked.

"Brothers."

"Sisters!"

"Parents."

"Teachers."

"Friends!"

"Friends are a problem?" Mrs. Levy asked innocently, but with a twinkle in her eye.

Everyone started to talk at once. Mrs. Levy folded her arms and waited. *Wow*, Debbie thought. *Look at her. She doesn't yell at us like a teacher. She just gets quiet and everyone gets a little embarrassed, like they're interrupting.*

"I see you all need to talk, but if you all talk at once, no one will get to hear you."

The girls quieted down. More hands went up.

"Sometimes someone will be your friend, and then one day they're just… not."

"Yeah," said another girl. "Like if they want to impress someone who doesn't like you." Debbie looked up. *Oh… I didn't know Hannah was here. Poor Hannah. I think she just lost her best friend.*

"Or if you were just tired that day and didn't talk to someone and they got all insulted."

"And sometimes someone bugs you so much you stop liking them."

Everyone laughed.

"I mean it," said the girl. "Like if they never bring pencils and pens to class and they always borrow and never return them." Debbie blushed. *Did I return the pen Leah loaned me yesterday?*

"Or if they get on a subject you're not interested in and they go on and on for days."

"Yeah! My friend's brother's getting married and all I've heard for a month is about the bride's dress and her mother's dress and this dress and that dress…"

Leah poked her. "Who does that sound like?" she whispered. Debbie smiled and didn't answer.

Now hands were waving. Some of the girls looked as though they were about to fall out of their seats.

"Lately," said one girl, "it seems like some of my friends have just… changed."

"How?" Mrs. Levy asked. "And," she added, "has anyone else felt like that?"

The noise level in the room shot up with the sound of chattering girls. There was a sea of waving hands.

"Some of my friends seem to change every day. They can be friendly one day and snobby the next."

"Or easy-going one day and cranky the next."

"It seems," said Mrs. Levy, and then she waited quietly again until everyone settled down. "It seems like you each need three or four books to start with."

Everyone laughed.

"But I see something interesting here. There is one person no one mentioned writing about! Can you guess who?" After a quiet moment, Debbie raised her hand hesitantly.

"G-d?" she asked.

Mrs. Levy looked at her, really looked at her. "I don't know you yet," she said. "But I think you have a sensitive soul. I hope we'll get to know each other better." Debbie felt so good when she heard that.

"G-d is definitely tied up with the answer I'm looking for. Who have we not mentioned yet?" There was still no answer, so Mrs. Levy slowly pointed to herself. A hand shot up.

"You!" said the girl. More laughter.

"I was pretending that I'm included. I would be if I was still keeping a journal. The answer I was looking for is 'ourselves.' No one yet mentioned writing about themselves."

"But... " one girl called out without raising her hand.

"Yes?" said Mrs. Levy. *Boy. She doesn't even say anything about calling out!*

"I don't need a whole book for that. I mean, I need one page to write: My name is Yocheved Sofer. I'm eleven and I have brown hair." Again there was laughter. Yocheved's face colored.

"I think I used the wrong word, Yocheved," said Mrs. Levy. "When I said to write about yourselves, I should have said 'your thoughts.' Besides just writing down what happened that day, you can write your thoughts about things. I think writing your thoughts helps you get to know yourself better, so they're really connected. You could write things like, 'Why can't everyone see I'm doing the best job I can?' or, 'Why does my mother misunderstand everything I say?' or... "

"Or 'I wish I didn't act like a baby when...'" interrupted someone else.

"Yes!" said Mrs. Levy, looking at the girl and beaming. She turned back to Yocheved. "Yocheved, did I make myself clear this time?"

Yocheved nodded, smiling.

"OK. Let's get focused for a minute. I used to always find it hard to start a new, empty journal, so I thought we could do it together. If you open your journals you'll find a pink envelope. There's a message just for you inside. You might want to read that before you start. Then, on the first page, write the purpose of this journal for you. When you get home and you get stuck about what to write, you can always re-read the first page and remember what to do. Write as if you're not writing at all, but talking—to a good friend just your age who always listens with interest to everything you say."

Debbie found her pink envelope and started to open it. *Wow. She spent all that time writing by hand to each one of these girls?* She looked at the paper and read the message.

"Inspiration is a spark that ignites you and sets you off like a rocket. It's what gets artists, inventors, or writers going. What did you see or hear that inspired you to do something new, or to change yourself?"

Debbie raised her hand. There was a puzzled look on her face.

"Yes, Debbie?" Mrs. Levy said.

"You said G-d was tied up in the answer. But we're writing about ourselves and **our** feelings and **our** problems."

Mrs. Levy's eyes connected so directly with Debbie's, and she had such a quiet, serious look on her face, that Debbie felt something turn around inside her.

"It's exactly connected, Debbie," she said. "When we write, and then read what we wrote and think about it, we get to know ourselves better. That 'self' you're getting to know is your soul—an actual part of G-d inside of you."

Debbie nodded and she didn't know why. *I don't get it, but I like it.*

She turned to her journal's first page. Normally, she hated being told what to write, but this time she felt slightly excited. Lots of times her head felt like it would explode from all of the thoughts zooming around inside. Maybe writing them down would help.

First, on the top right-hand corner, she wrote her name and address. Then she skipped some lines. Her pen hovered above the page for a few moments. Finally, it touched down and scribbled down the line. "When I write in this journal," Debbie wrote, "I'm really writing to myself. I know who I am. Debbie Solomon, 11 years old. I'm nice and fun to be with. I'm good at English and terrible at math. I'm serious about the swim team and I'm pretty good at it. I even made the finals for the junior freestyle race last season. What I don't know so well is this: I'm a Jewish girl. What is so special about that?"

Debbie looked around for a minute, biting on the end of her pencil. Girls were closing their books, but she didn't really notice.

"In this book, I will write things I can't say to anyone else. Maybe then my thoughts will slow down, and when I read what I wrote, I'll be able to figure out what to do about it."

"Okay," Mrs. Levy broke in, "that's great for this week. You can do more at home. Write as much as you like, but write at least once a week. If any of you go through the whole book before your Bat Mitzvah, your prize is a new book to write in." Everyone laughed.

"Also, before you go," she continued, "inside your gold folders are some things that I want you to read. There's a schedule of Club meetings and a description of our activities. There's some general information about becoming a Bat Mitzvah, too—you can read that at home so you can give it more time. Most of all, there's a list of jobs that all of you will take turns doing. We'll rotate."

"Each week, two of you will give a short talk about an experience or thought that ties into your lives in a Jewish way. Who will do that next week?"

Mrs. Levy began reading through the list of jobs and choosing girls to fill them for the following week. Sometimes no one volunteered and she had to choose someone. "We're in this together," she said. "If it's hard for you, call me. Here's my number."

As the assignments went on, Debbie read down the list. Give a talk about the meaning of Bat Mitzvah. Debbie shuddered. *I don't know what to say!* Secretary. *Doesn't sound too bad. Just take notes and hand out copies the next week.* Hostesses to set up refreshments and help clean up afterward. *I couldn't stay late! What about my swim practice?* Mistress of Ceremonies to introduce speakers and activities. *Leah would love that one.* She read on. "Each week," she read, "the latest Bat Mitzvah will be presented with a gift." *Nice.*

Debbie looked up to hear Mrs. Levy speaking again.

"... and I hope that we'll learn about being a Jewish girl and the responsibilities that come with becoming a Bat Mitzvah. Judaism has so much to say about it. For next week, I'm going to be asking you what you expect to happen at your Bat Mitzvah and afterward, so maybe you can start thinking about your answer ahead of time. That's all for today."

Everyone was instantly chattering to each other, gathering their things, putting on coats, but just for a minute before Leah descended on her, Debbie sat quietly. *This doesn't sound bad at all.*

CHAPTER FOUR

ebbie and Leah rushed out of the meeting. They had about seven minutes to go the two blocks to the Jewish Community Center to warm up for the swim-meet. This was not just any swim-meet. Their opponents this week were last year's junior champions. That meant that Debbie would be racing in the freestyle event against Rachel Levine, the Rachel Levine who held the top record.

Debbie's time was good, the best on her team in freestyle—good enough to have been invited to race in last year's junior finals, but nothing she did in training could give her the Levine Power Stroke. Still, Debbie had worked hard in practice this year and she had shaved nearly four seconds off her time. Maybe Rachel would have an off day.

"Debbie, I just know you can beat her," Leah said, as if

reading her thoughts. "Sure, she's all muscle, but you're lighter, and your stroke is just as strong as hers."

Debbie laughed. "Leah, you're the best cheerleader! Thanks for the pep talk. I wish I was a diver. You don't have to do anything once you're in the water."

"Hey," Leah countered with a pout, "don't knock divers. It's what we do before we get in the water that really counts."

Just then, the girls reached the locker room.

"It's about time!" Mrs. Brown called. "I thought you said you'd only miss a small part of practice."

"Uh, sorry, Mrs. Brown," Leah murmured, for once subdued.

"Well, you've missed warm-ups, but maybe if you hurry you can still get a few in," Mrs. Brown said, looking at the clock on the wall. "Better hurry, champs!" she added with a grin as Debbie and Leah got into their swimsuits.

Debbie leaned forward. Her knees slightly bent, she gripped the edge of the pool with her toes. Her long arms stretched out behind her. She always loved the tense excitement of this moment. Spectators leaned forward in the stands. Debbie smiled to herself, knowing that her mother and Miri were out there somewhere, eyes glued to her. Mrs. Brown stood with the other coaches along the far end of the pool. The black lane markers stood out beneath the motionless aqua-blue water. A hush filled the air.

Debbie turned her head both ways to see the racers

lined up on either side of her. She saw Jennifer two lanes over. There was Rachel Levine in the very next position. Rachel always looked so deep in concentration, never looking around at the competition, never doubting her ability to win.

Debbie held her breath. As the starter's pistol went off, she inhaled sharply, forcefully swung her arms forward, and pushed with all of her might. She broke the water at a sharp angle, barely creating a splash. She glided beneath the surface for a moment, then she began kicking furiously, her arms shoving the water with hard strokes.

She swiveled back into position after the first turn and, for a split second, raised her head toward Rachel's lane. Debbie gasped. They were nearly neck and neck. "Wow!" she thought to herself, "I'm making great time." She knew that Rachel's main strategy was to hold something back for the extra push that she always gave at the end of the race. "I'll just keep up," Debbie told herself as she made her second flip-turn.

Debbie was feeling great at the halfway mark. She sliced through the water, putting everything she had into the race. "More, more, more!" she coached herself. "I can do it!" She knew her teammates and the people in the stands were probably jumping up and down and waving their arms by now. "Go, Debbie!" they screamed. "You can do it!"

It was the final lap. Fatigue coursed through her limbs. Debbie was tempted to ease her pace, but she pushed herself even harder. She didn't glance at Rachel or at the end of the lane—she just swam her strongest. She was going for it, pumping her arms and legs faster than ever before.

Suddenly, she felt the pool's concrete edge. Debbie grabbed the edge and popped her head up. She whipped off her goggles. Her breath came in jagged gasps. Shouts surrounded her, but she couldn't make out the words. Turning to her left, she saw Rachel next to her. Rachel's limbs were firm and muscular. Her athletic features had an open, healthy look. Rachel pulled off her swim cap and shook out her short hair. She was straining to see her time posted on the board across the pool. Debbie looked up at the board and found her own time posted. What she saw made her whoop with glee. She had dropped another second off her time.

"A tie?" Rachel said in a disappointed voice.

Debbie shrieked. "A tie!" She looked around the pool for her teammates. "I tied?" A giant smile came over her face. She turned to Rachel, her arm outstretched. Rachel stood dripping, her large blue eyes downcast. Rachel accepted Debbie's vigorous handshake quietly.

"Great race, Debbie," Rachel said with obvious disappointment.

Debbie couldn't stop grinning. "Thanks, Rachel! Your competition gave me my best time ever!" Debbie wanted to hug her, but did not make the move.

Debbie's heart was pounding faster than during the hardest part of the race. Her head felt light, like she wanted to jump and shout. She had never been so excited. Suddenly, Debbie felt herself being lifted out of the water by her teammates. Everyone was cheering. Debbie wiped her eyes. She couldn't believe it. Debbie Solomon tied with Rachel Levine, the fastest junior swimmer!

This is my greatest day ever! I can't wait for the finals. I'll take home the trophy this year!

Debbie's face was still flushed with victory when she met her mother and Miri near the pool. She felt so generous that she even gave a surprised Miri a big hug. Her mother was smiling broadly, and greeted Debbie with outstretched arms. *Mom always comes for me. Every time.* Debbie held on a long time. She felt almost reluctant to kiss her mother goodbye and run to meet up with Leah, but the two always walked home together from meets so they could talk about their scores. She knew her mother didn't mind. She smiled and tousled Miri's head. "Mom, I'll be home soon, OK? We just want to walk." Debbie's mother nodded understandingly.

"This is one of the best days of my life!" Debbie said to Leah as they walked through their city neighborhood. The two chattered excitedly about the swim-meet. They would have continued their conversation all the way home, had they not walked past the windows of the Unique Boutique shop. What they saw there stopped them in their tracks.

Right there in the window, impossible to miss, was The Dress. The perfect Bat Mitzvah dress. It seemed to shout at them, "I'm It!"

"Wow!" the girls said in unison. They pushed open the door and made a beeline for the dress. A tag dangled off its gorgeous sleeve. Debbie picked up the tag and moaned. The price, written in the thick black letters of a magic marker, taunted her.

"Oh, no!" Debbie moaned. "No way will my parents go for this. Even if I win the junior championship!"

"I don't know, Debs. It is a special occasion," Leah said hopefully, but with a wink. "Like Mrs. Levy would say, we're becoming part of this great line of Jewish women and all."

"Nice try," Debbie said dejectedly, turning away to scout out the other, more modestly priced racks.

Leah, however, went to the expensive rack and pulled a copy of The Dress off a hanger. She held The Dress against herself as she checked out her reflection in the full-length mirror. She smiled and twirled as the crisp taffeta swayed in the air, making her chocolate brown eyes and freckles dance. "This dress could make anyone feel like a winner!" she declared as she turned in front of the mirror. She handed the dress over to Debbie, "See for yourself!"

Leah took the dress with a grin, and held it up to herself in front of the mirror. Right away she thought of her mother.

"My mother would never go for this."

"Come on, Deb. Why not?" Leah's voice had a playful whine.

"She calls this loud, like clothes make noise or something. She likes things she calls quiet, you know, not real show-offy."

"But it is a great dress."

Debbie looked at the mirror and her eyes were drawn to the shine of the taffeta and the rich colors of the print and the princess sleeves. She couldn't take her eyes off the dress.

"It is beautiful," she said ruefully. *But the colors are all wrong for me.* She couldn't tell Leah what she really thought. She didn't want to spoil the moment.

"Hey, Deb," Leah called out, "I've got a great idea!"

Debbie smiled nervously. *Uh oh.* Too often, Leah's "great ideas" ended up with someone getting into trouble. Like the time Leah decided they should skip school instead of facing a science quiz for which neither of them had prepared. The girls left home as usual that day, but spent the whole day at the park and the mall. It was fun for a while, but Debbie felt so guilty that she had a terrible stomachache the whole time. Of course, their science teacher put two and two together and figured out that something was suspicious with both of them missing on a quiz day. They tried to look innocent when they got home that afternoon, but their parents had already received a phone call from school about what they'd done. Not only were they each given an "F" on the quiz, but their parents grounded them both for two weeks. When they returned to school, Leah seemed nonchalant, but Debbie couldn't face the science teacher for a week.

"I don't know about your great ideas," Debbie replied ruefully.

"Don't worry so much, Deb," Leah laughed. "I just thought of a way you could get this dress."

"Nothing illegal!" Debbie giggled.

"No. Of course I wouldn't do anything like that!" Leah whispered, her eye on the saleslady standing behind the counter at the other end of the store. "But listen to me. Tell your parents The Dress is only sixty dollars. They'll definitely go for that. Then, borrow your father's charge card to pick it up, and by the time the bill comes in, you will have already worn it for your Bat Mitzvah. If they start to complain, you can cry or something. They'll be mad for a minute or two, but you'll still have the dress!"

"That's a terrible idea!" Debbie exclaimed. "I couldn't do that! Do you know what kind of trouble I'd be in then? Anyway, my Bat Mitzvah is months from now. The credit card bill will come in before then. Besides, Leah," Debbie looked straight at her friend. "That's just plain stealing."

"Yeah, you've got a point," Leah said as she carefully hung The Dress back up on the rack. "Anyway, do you always have to be such a goody-goody?"

Debbie's face turned red. She knew what Leah meant but she didn't get the point of doing stupid things that would just get her in trouble and make everyone around her unhappy. Maybe she doesn't expect she'd get in trouble. Leah was the only girl at home. Her two oldest siblings were grown, and her brother was always busy with basketball. Her parents were older than Debbie's were, and they lavished attention on Leah. *She always expects to get what she wants.*

Sometimes when Leah suggested one of her schemes, Debbie felt so torn. Part of her felt thrilled, but then she'd realize she couldn't possibly go along with it.

Maybe Leah isn't such a good influence. But whenever I try to spend time with other girls, Leah gets mad. And anyway, I don't want to lose her friendship. No other girl's so much fun to be around. Debbie worried that Leah would meet another girl who wasn't such a goody-goody and drop her like a hot potato. It was almost worth going along with Leah just to keep her friendship. *I wonder what Mrs. Levy would say.*

And why did Leah's crazy planning make her really want that dress? Right then the dress seemed so beautiful, almost irresistible.

Leah broke into Debbie's thoughts. "All right, Deb. Your Bat Mitzvah isn't until the spring. But just think about my idea. Come on, let's go."

The girls gave The Dress backward glances as they left the store. "Your parents will probably get it for you," Debbie said to Leah, forcing a smile. "Besides, we couldn't possibly get the same dress, and it goes much better with your coloring. I'm too pale. It'll be gorgeous on you." Debbie felt slightly sad and relieved at the same time.

When she got home, she was met with the delicious

smell of chicken in the oven. When her father got home, he gave her the biggest smile and swept her into his arms. At the dinner table the atmosphere was joyful. Debbie could see that her parents were proud of her. She looked at her father, who sat so tall next to her petite mother. His light brown hair did not quite manage to cover the place on top of his head where it was thinning out and his balding head shone beneath. As he smiled at her, many fine lines stood out at the outer corners of his wide-set, chocolate eyes. *Smile lines. It's because he does it so much.* She sat back, satisfied.

Finally, full of the family joy and good food, Debbie excused herself. Somehow, behind the good feelings, something made Debbie want to be alone. She closed her bedroom door behind her and, without thinking, reached for her Bat Mitzvah Club journal that lay neglected on her desk. She stretched out on her stomach on her bed and began to write. "I wonder," she wrote, "if Leah would have considered tricking her parents into buying that dress if I suggested it to her? This is my biggest secret: Sometimes I wonder if I really want to be Leah's friend."

CHAPTER FIVE

The rest of the week passed in a glow. At every odd moment Debbie relived that sweet moment of victory and felt her teammates lifting her out of the water. She did have one small problem that kept bothering her. She wanted to settle comfortably back into her regular school routine, but she felt a little leery around Leah.

One night that week she wrote in her journal, "Why do Leah's crazy ideas make me want to do them?"

It seemed like no time before Tuesday came around again. She and Leah made sure they were not late to the Bat Mitzvah Club meeting. Debbie came with her bathing suit, cap, and goggles stuffed into her backpack. "I hope this doesn't go overtime," she whispered to Leah. "Yeah," Leah replied, "or Mrs. Brown will have our heads." The two quickly found seats together.

Mrs. Levy began by showing them four pictures of the same woman at different ages; as an infant, a child, an adult, and as an old woman. "Before we start, I'd like you all to spread out and write a short story about this woman or a short description of her. Just a few paragraphs. Let me know a few of her thoughts and feelings." Debbie was mystified. *What does this have to do with my Bat Mitzvah?*

For eight of the ten minutes that they had to write, Debbie chewed on the end of her pencil. Finally she wrote a few sentences, then stopped because the time was up. Anyway, she didn't know what else to write.

For the next few minutes Debbie listened to several girls reading their stories about the woman. Most were really imaginative. She hoped Mrs. Levy wouldn't ask her to read. She was embarrassed that she had so little to say.

Leah leaned over and whispered, "What did you write?"

"Not much. I couldn't think of anything."

"I made her a swimmer."

Debbie giggled. "Senior citizen freestyle champion," she said.

Mrs. Levy was talking to her but she had not heard. She looked up just as Mrs. Levy said, "Do you want to read yours?" Debbie blushed.

"I... couldn't think of something to write."

"You don't have to read it if you don't want."

"I... I guess I could read it, but it's just a few sentences, not a story at all." She silently cleared her throat and began to read out loud.

"I used to be a child. Now I am old. But inside me, I still feel like a child. I wish I could ride a bicycle again. I know

I still know how."

"More words don't necessarily make it better," Mrs. Levy said. "Sometimes so much can be said in just a few sentences. You made me feel as if I knew this woman."

Debbie smiled. "Tell me, Debbie," said Mrs. Levy. "What is this woman?"

"I... I don't know. I don't understand."

"Who would like to say?"

"A woman," said one girl.

"A mother."

"A grandmother."

"An American."

"Wait," Mrs. Levy said. "You're telling me about her roles. But what is at the deepest part of what she is?"

Debbie thought for a moment and then raised her hand.

"She's...she's a body. I mean, skin and bones and blood and... stuff like that."

Mrs. Levy looked at the pictures. Each one was so different. "Which body is she?" Everyone laughed. *I wish everyone didn't always have to laugh at everything.*

Mrs. Levy looked at her intently. "A person's appearance changes, doesn't it? Are you the same as you were ten years ago?"

"No," Debbie said, stifling her own laugh. She was thinking of her baby picture on the windowsill at home, thankful that she didn't have those rolls of fat any more. *Boy, that would sure slow me down in the water.*

"Are you going to look the same twenty years from now?"

"No." Thinking of those changes made her face get red again. *But I hope I look as nice as you.*

"Are you still the same person inside? Are you going to be the same person twenty years from now?"

"No... well, in a way, yes."

"If the outside of us changes so much, what stays the same? What is it that we call "me" that never changes?" Mrs. Levy said this to everyone.

Yocheved said thoughtfully, "I think it's our soul." No one was thinking about raising hands anymore. Mrs. Levy didn't seem to notice.

Mrs. Levy smiled at her. "A soul," she said. "Since it is an extension of G-d, right inside of us, we can call it a G-dly soul, can't we? Most people think they have to search everywhere to find G-d. They even wonder if He's there, when He's right inside of us. That's where we can look first."

"Now," she said. "I'll tell you what this has to do with a Bat Mitzvah." Debbie felt as if Mrs. Levy had read her thoughts. "Your Bat Mitzvah is the time when your G-dly soul becomes complete. That's what it means when people tell you that becoming a Bat Mitzvah means you're now a woman, a grown-up, full-fledged member of the Jewish religion. It's like your soul has been waiting all this time to really show itself and now it saturates you like... like water fills a sponge."

"So what does this grown-up soul want?" Mrs. Levy's face was questioning. There was silence. "I'll give you a hint. If it's an extension of G-d, then we can ask, 'What does G-d want?' and it will be, in a way, the same question, won't it? So, what does G-d want of us?"

"To be good," one girl said.

"To listen to our parents."

"To do good in school."

Mrs. Levy looked around. "Really, all your answers can be put in one word: *mitzvot*. Mitzvot are the things G-d tells us to do in the Torah. Some mitzvot are specific things to observe, such as keeping Shabbat and the Jewish holidays. Other mitzvot are things to believe or a general way to behave, such as believing in G-d, or honoring parents."

"Doing our mitzvot is what G-d wants, and what makes our soul happy. Really. It feels good. You'll feel that special feeling, too—wanting mitzvot, and that good feeling when you do them—in the best, biggest way right after your Bat Mitzvah. You'll see!"

Mrs. Levy turned and picked up her papers in a way that made it clear she was finished speaking. *She never talks long enough to get boring.*

"Now may I have some volunteers to help run next week's class?"

At first, no one wanted to offer, but Mrs. Levy assured the girls that by the end of the year everyone will have done all of the jobs. She also said that those girls who volunteered early would get extra help from her. Several girls raised their hands.

Debbie spoke up. "I could be a hostess."

"Why don't you run the next meeting?" Mrs. Levy suggested. "You can be the M.C."

"I couldn't run the meeting! Anyway, not this early. After swim season ends, I'll do it," she promised. She groaned to herself. *Ohhh. Why did I do that?*

"I'll remember that," Mrs. Levy said with a smile. "Okay, then, why don't you and Leah be our hostesses?" Leah looked at Debbie in amazement.

"Okay," the girls answered.

Debbie thought for a second. "But Mrs. Levy," she said.

"Yes?"

"We can set up, but we can't stay late to clean up because we will already be late for swim practice."

"Would someone like to volunteer to be partners for the hostess job and clean up next week so Debbie and Leah can get to swim practice?"

Several girls gamely raised their hand. *Problem solved.* Debbie turned and smiled at them.

"Hey, Deb," Leah leaned over and whispered with new respect. "Not bad—we'll get first shot at the refreshments!"

CHAPTER SIX

Debbie and Leah slowly stood up and left the class. "Wow, Leah," Debbie said. "Who ever thought there was so much about Bat Mitzvah that we didn't know about?"

"Yeah, and wait until we get to the part about giving a speech for the guests," Leah retorted. "I don't know. It's interesting, and it might be fun to be a hostess, but all the soul stuff sounds weird to me." She pushed back her black velvet headband, trying to control her unruly curls. "How come we never heard about a G-dly soul before?"

The girls turned the corner toward Debbie's house. Leah's parents had concert tickets that night and wouldn't be home until late, so Debbie had invited Leah to spend the night. "Can you believe your parents let you spend the night on a school night?" Debbie said with amazement.

"And I'm just as surprised that my parents agreed."

"Sure," Leah said ruefully. "We had to make a zillion promises."

"Worth it?" Debbie asked.

"Worth it!" Leah answered. "I think maybe... I think it might be because of the Bat Mitzvah Club and because our Bat Mitzvahs are coming. I think they feel they should trust us more. At least, that's what I keep telling them."

"Maybe our parents pushed us to go to this Bat Mitzvah class," Debbie said, "because they wondered if all we think about being Jewish is Chanukah presents and a big Bat Mitzvah party."

"And Hebrew verbs!" Leah said, wincing. "*Yeladim!*" she called out in her best imitation of an adult with a heavy Hebrew accent. She clapped her hands twice. "*Zman avar! Ani...* Oh no! Seet daown pleeeese!"

Debbie was laughing already. "You sound just like Mrs. Bar Yam!" She turned to her friend. "So what did your parents say about that gorgeous dress, anyway?"

Leah grinned. "I'm breaking them into the idea slowly. But I think they'll give in. Especially if you help me get an 'A' on that English assignment that's due tomorrow."

"And what do I get if I do?" Debbie teased.

"Another good deed, Deb. Isn't that what you care about?" Leah poked her friend. Debbie frowned at her. "Okay, okay, don't get insulted. A good deed and my friendship—though I saw you acting like you're Rachel Levine's best friend, so I don't know if you even need my friendship anymore," Leah said, faking a self-pitying tone.

Debbie didn't look convinced.

"Leah, don't you have more than one friend?" She wanted Leah to understand that it's OK. She wanted Leah to admit her jealousy was silly. But still Leah wouldn't answer the question.

"All right, all right. Maybe I'll find time in my busy schedule to help you out in math."

Debbie sighed, and then inwardly shrugged her shoulders. "Now we're talking," Debbie said and grinned at her friend.

"You seem less jumpy, Deb," her father commented that night at dinner. "Did you have those pre-Bat Mitzvah Club jitters, too, Leah?" he asked, smiling.

"Are you kidding?" Leah answered. "I locked myself in my room for two nights during dinner and only came out for dessert."

"So the Club meetings are not so bad?" Mrs. Solomon asked. "I haven't heard much about it."

"No, Mom. They're not bad at all. It's just that I have to be late to swim practice every time and I can't explain why to Mrs. Brown."

"Why don't you just tell her the truth?"

Debbie's face reddened. "Mom... you just don't understand."

"I think Debbie doesn't want to make Mrs. Brown jealous of the Club meetings," Leah piped in. "You know how seriously she takes swim practice."

"Mrs. Brown or Debbie?" Mr. Solomon asked.

"Mrs. Brown. Or, I mean, both, I guess," Leah said. Debbie rolled her eyes. "Well," Leah went on, "we've got a good chance in the finals and we don't want to disappoint her."

"You know what, Debbie," her father said with a smile. "I think I'd like to give Mrs. Brown a call myself and see how the team's doing. Maybe I'll let her know you'll be giving her a call to work out a way to make up your missed practices."

"Good luck," Debbie said in a skeptical tone. She folded her arms in front of her. "Mrs. Brown is really into the team this year." She looked at her father's confused expression and felt bad. "Daddy," she said in a softer tone. "I know you like me learning about being Jewish, but it's hard when the club takes time away from other stuff."

"You must make up your practices," Debbie's father said to her. "I want you to have a strong mind and a strong body." Debbie shifted in her seat and felt uncomfortable. *Uh oh. Am I going to get a lecture with Leah here?*

Debbie's mother looked thoughtful. "What would Mrs. Levy say?" she asked.

"She'd probably say to look at the problems some famous Jewish women faced and see how they solved them." Debbie said this in a put-on, bored tone of voice. Leah giggled.

"Other people's troubles always seem so different from

your own," her father agreed. "But you look at people and you might see a lot of similarities. People aren't that different."

Debbie's mother leaned forward. "Debbie, why don't you go visit your grandmother on Sunday? Ask her if you can look through her really old photo albums. I think she'll have some interesting stories to tell you."

Mr. Solomon looked surprised. "Sarah, are you sure you want Debbie to get into that? She's only eleven." He paused. Some kind of electricity seemed to pass between her parents' eyes, as if they could talk without words. Mr. Solomon looked surprised, and concerned about something that he obviously did not want to voice. "Come to the kitchen for a minute," Mr. Solomon requested in a low voice.

Debbie frowned. *What's such a big secret? I've gone through Grandma Eva's pictures a hundred times and heard the stories a hundred more. But the way they're acting, you'd think there was a real mystery!*

Debbie thought about the stories Grandma Eva told when she traced her life from a small Russian village to America. She knew times were hard for Grandma Eva's family and for a lot of others even before Hitler came to power in Germany in 1933. But gradually Grandma Eva's family knew they had to escape. News was beginning to trickle in about what Hitler was doing to Jews in the countries that he conquered, and Grandma Eva's father felt certain that he would try to conquer Russia as well. Her father's friends argued with him, because Hitler had signed a treaty with Russia and pledged peace, but Grandma Eva's father secretly made plans to get away. Grandma Eva was eleven years old when she had to leave her beloved home, her school and her friends. They ran off in the middle of the night with her brother and their family, bringing only the things they could carry with them. There were no good-byes. Using fake passports, they took a long, frightening train ride to cousins in France. But they could not stay there.

Her parents could only get two visas for America, so they put Grandma Eva and her brother on a ship to America. Debbie smiled as she thought of how seasick Grandma was on the ship. *Every time she tells me the story she turns a little green.* Debbie could almost see Grandma Eva's face the way it looked when she was recounting the endless back-and-forth motion of the ship, the crowded berths where she and her brother squeezed onto a bunk bed in a big, noisy area filled with screaming babies, restless children and seasick parents. Grandma Eva and her brother struggled to sleep every night of the two-week voyage, certain that they would never see their parents again.

Their uncle and aunt and three cousins met them at the boat. They tried to make the two young refugees feel at home in their small apartment, and Eva tried to be helpful. Debbie imagined the effort it must have taken to pretend to be cheerful and useful when, inside, Grandma

Eva was terrified that her parents were in danger. She stayed busy with her English classes as well, but she only felt happy again when her mother and father finally made it to America. What joy they had, celebrating their miraculous survival. How happy the family was to be together again!

Debbie knew the whole menu for her great grandparents "Welcome to America" party. Grandma was so proud that her aunt was able to serve such fancy food during wartime when so many things were scarce or rationed. There was roast and potatoes and homemade challah and fresh salads and cookies. Her uncle brought out his homemade wine. Debbie could just picture the scene with the table laden with delicious food and the children wrapped safely in their parents' arms. Thinking about it, she could almost smell the roast cooking. For a moment, Debbie felt she was Eva, and could almost feel the warm softness of her mother's arms that were so sorely missed.

Leah broke into Debbie's daydream. "Hey, what's the big secret with your parents?"

"Yeah," Miri added. "'How long are they going to stay in there? Does this mean I can take thirds on the apple pie?"

Just then Mr. and Mrs. Solomon came back in from the kitchen. Mrs. Solomon smiled as she sat back down in her place at the table. "Debbie," she said. "We just talked to Grandma, and she's planning on having you visit Sunday afternoon. Okay?"

Debbie nodded, and looked keenly at her mother.

What's going on here?

"I'm coming, too," Miri chimed in.

"No," Mr. Solomon said. "This has to do with Debbie's Bat Mitzvah. Besides, I thought you had a date with Becky."

"I don't have to go," Miri said hopefully.

"Keep your date, Miri," Mr. Solomon said.

Debbie and Leah eyed each other. "What's going on?" she asked her parents. She turned to her mother. "Why do you want me to look at Grandma's old pictures?"

"Oh, well, I think it's time for you to get to know more about your family."

"In honor of your Bat Mitzvah," Debbie's father added. Debbie wasn't so sure.

"Maybe you'll dig up something at Grandmother's that will help you with your Bat Mitzvah speech," he added.

Debbie and Leah groaned in unison. "Don't remind us!" Leah said. "Debbie's the one who always gets an 'A' in creative writing. I don't know what I'll do."

"You know I'll help you," Debbie said, then added with a sly smile, "for a price."

Everyone laughed. The girls got up to gather the supper dishes together. "Well," Leah said. "Maybe the microphone will break down just at the right moment—at the beginning of my speech!"

CHAPTER SEVEN

unday couldn't have come soon enough for Debbie. She woke up early, threw on some jeans and a sweater, and bounded down the stairs from the second floor. She had a spring in her step as she walked into the kitchen. Her father grabbed his heart and staggered backward in mock surprise as Debbie walked in. "Could it already be noon?" he asked, as he turned to look at the clock above the stove. "You mean I missed my tennis game?"

"Very funny, Dad," Debbie said, and then she kissed his cheek. She poured herself some orange juice and put two slices of bread into the toaster.

"I don't always sleep late on Sundays, do I?" she said doubtfully.

"Of course not!" her father chuckled as he settled back

down to his coffee and the hefty Sunday paper. "Only once a week!"

Debbie laughed. "Oh, Daddy," she said. "I just know Grandma's expecting me and I don't want her to have to wait all day."

"That's very considerate of you, my dear," her father said. He reached over to feel her forehead. "Are you feeling okay?"

"Daddy!" Debbie squealed. Then she paused and said thoughtfully, "I'm almost Bat Mitzvah. Mrs. Levy said that's when I have to do my own mitzvot and not wait for someone to ask. But I am a little sleepy... " Debbie put her head down on the table.

"Good girl," her father said, pulling her to her feet. "I'm so glad that class is doing so much for you. And you've only been late to a couple of swim practices."

"Yeah, but I think Mrs. Brown is being extra hard on me during my make-ups. She says I've got to get in the hours or I can't be on the team. I've never done so many laps in my life."

"Is it worth it?" Debbie's father asked in a serious tone. Debbie was surprised that he would ask that question.

"Well... " Debbie said, popping out her toast before it got burned, "I've always felt Jewish anyway, like it's just what I am. I don't need the Bat Mitzvah Club for that."

"You always felt Jewish—even in public school?"

"Sure. Well... maybe I used to feel a little left out around December, but we always had such nice Chanukahs that I didn't feel I was really missing out."

"Then are you glad we switched you to a Jewish school?"

"Yes! The change made me feel so at home—I mean, after I got to know people and caught up with the classes."

"So… tell me what you're getting out of the Bat Mitzvah Club."

Debbie looked up at the ceiling sort of sideways, like she was thinking. "Well… I feel like, for the first time, I'm learning why I'm Jewish. The school teaches us plenty, but not that. It's like, if you really think about being Jewish every day, I mean, try to make everything you do Jewish, then you become a better person and… " Debbie's voice trailed off. It was hard for her to finish the sentence.

"And?" her father was waiting.

"You feel close to… to G-d."

She turned to her father. "You get what I'm saying?"

"If that's what you're getting out of the Club, then… can I come, too?"

"Oh, Daddy!" Debbie blushed.

"That's really beautiful."

"I'm just saying what Mrs. Levy told us in class. But it does make you think."

"Yes, it does," her father agreed.

Debbie swept toast crumbs into her empty plate, put the plate in the sink, and headed for the door. "If Grandma phones, tell her I'm on my way," she told her father. "See ya," she called, pulling on her jacket. "I gotta go. There's

Aunt Sophie to give me a ride to Grandma's. She's going that way to go shopping."

Half an hour later, Aunt Sophie stopped her small, red Ford in front of Grandma Eva's apartment building and let Debbie off. Debbie always gripped her jacket a little closer to her when she came to Grandma's part of town. Everyone told her it used to be as nice a neighborhood as her own, but that was when her mother was little. Her grandmother's friends still lived here, and, especially after Grandpa Jake passed away years ago, her grandmother just felt more comfortable staying. "This is my home," she said. "Must I lose this, too?"

From time to time, Debbie's parents invited Grandma to move into their house, but Grandma always said she liked her freedom. "What if you start grounding me for coming in late?" she would ask with a laugh.

When the elevator reached the top floor and the doors opened, her grandmother was standing right there, waiting for her. Debbie leaned down to kiss her and filled her nostrils with the scent of soap, Grandma's special perfume, and warm baked goods. Then she stepped back and took in her grandmother's blue eyes, her small nose and delicate mouth and thought for the first time that this must be similar to how her mother would eventually grow to look. "Come in, come in! I'm so happy to see you!" Debbie let herself be led by the hand into her grandmother's immaculate apartment.

"Ohh, I missed you, Grandma," Debbie declared as she lingered for a moment in her grandmother's embrace. *No one else feels like Grandma Eva. The softest skin, and... cookies!* Debbie settled on the couch next to Grandma Eva and reached for the cookie plate that was already waiting as always.

Debbie caught her grandmother's watchful eye. She knew what her grandmother was waiting to hear. Debbie pronounced the blessing *"Borei Minei Mezonot,"* and looked for Grandma Eva's smiling acknowledgement. She learned to say the blessing from her grandmother right here on this sofa eating one of these cookies. *Maybe that's why Grandma Eva's cookies taste so special.*

"Thanks," Debbie said, munching her favorite, an oat-meal-raisin cookie. "Mmmm, so good. We have your recipe, but the cookies never taste the same when we make them. How have you been feeling, Grandma?"

"Oy, Devorah," Grandma said, calling Debbie by her Hebrew name. "At my age, every day's a gift. But the best present of all is your visits. And your mother tells me this one isn't just a social call."

Debbie nodded. "I kind of figured that out. I think Mom and Dad wanted me to come see you because of my Bat Mitzvah. You know I've been going to classes." Debbie was quiet for a moment. "Tell me about your Bat Mitzvah, Grandma." Debbie loved to hear her grandmother's sto-ries. They made her feel as if they were happening before her eyes.

Her grandmother smiled, although sadly, it seemed. "I remember my Bat Mitzvah well. Who could ever forget? I was far away from my parents and from any life I'd known. I turned twelve on the ship traveling to America, you know."

"You did?" Debbie exclaimed. "I never knew that!"

"It was just me and my brother," Grandma Eva slowly recounted. "I was so seasick and homesick that I forgot all about my birthday, but my brother remembered. One afternoon, he pulled me from the bunk where I was buried under musty, scratchy blankets. I was trying to sleep and make the trip pass quicker. He took my hand and pulled me out onto the swaying deck. Then he led me around to a small room that served as the ship's synagogue. I was a mess—there was so little opportunity to bathe or wash my hair on the ship—and I felt embarrassed to go into that room. But my brother whispered that I looked fine and opened up the door. As soon as we got inside, I couldn't help it. I started to cry. Everything I saw made me think of my parents."

Debbie sat back on the couch and Grandma Eva sat back, too, putting an arm around her. "The rabbis there reminded me so much of home. They were huddled around their big books, discussing passages from the Torah. For a moment I forgot I was on that miserable ship. I thought I was home again, watching my father on a Shabbat afternoon while he studied the Torah in the synagogue with his friends, trying to follow parts of the conversation but getting lost in all the different voices with their opinions. I used to sit on a bench in the corner and wait for your great-grandfather to notice me. When he did, he'd slowly shake hands with his friends, gather up his prayer shawl, and take my hand for the walk home for lunch."

Grandma's eyes looked far away. "We'd get home to a feast. We had soup and chicken and my mother's strudels. All the family was there! Everyone! Aunts and uncles and little cousins who'd chase each other around the table and under our feet. I'll never forget it," she said softly. "I was sure life would go on like that forever, so that even when I grew up and got married and moved into my own house down the road, I'd still sit around my parents' big table..."

Debbie had heard about life in Grandma Eva's village a hundred times before. It always made Debbie sad to think that that whole life, the village and everything in it, had been destroyed in the war. It was hard to imagine what her father said—that there weren't any more Jews left at all in that part of the world.

"So where was I, Devorah'leh?" Grandma Eva asked. "Oh, yes, on that smelly ship. Well, my brother sat me on a bench and reached into his jacket for a package. 'Mama and Papa made me promise to give you this today,' he said. Then he leaned over to kiss my forehead. He said, 'Happy birthday—and Happy Bat Mitzvah.'

"You understand that right then we wondered if we would ever see our parents again. We were just two children alone on the sea, twelve and fourteen years old. I held the package for a moment and tried to feel my mother's hands as she'd folded and taped the paper wrapping. I carefully opened the box, and inside I found a pair of silver candlesticks—those that you see right over there."

She waved her hand toward her china cabinet. There, on a gleaming silver tray, was a pair of candlesticks. "Every Friday, just before nightfall, I light the candles in those candlesticks." Grandma Eva sat back on the couch and looked in the direction of the china cabinet, seemingly lost among the memories that the candlesticks held for her.

"There was a note with it," she continued. "I lost it somewhere along the way. But I remember my mother's elegant, old-fashioned handwriting. She wrote:

> To my darling Eva. Now you are a Jewish woman and it is your job to remember the Sabbath properly. We are thinking of you every minute that we are apart. Today I am especially praying for you—that you are safe and that, wherever you are, you will continue to grow to be a fine Jewish woman.

Grandma Eva squeezed Debbie's arm. "The war changed so many things. My brother and I had passports that said that my uncle was really my father. My parents were hoping to make the journey to America to us, but they did not have the papers to allow them to come. With the terrible danger they were in, getting the proper papers was only one of their problems. I remember thinking that what my mother really meant, but didn't write, was that they hoped that they would make it through that terrible war."

Grandma Eva drifted into silence for a long moment. She drew a breath and continued her story. "Then, one of the rabbis waved me over. I stood before him and he blessed me in Hebrew, just the way my father would every Friday night: 'May the L-rd bless you and keep you. May the L-rd make His face shine upon you and be gracious to you. May the L-rd turn His face toward you and grant you peace.'

"The rabbi asked me to sit down and pointed to one of the benches that were bolted to the floor. He told me some things about becoming a Bat Mitzvah. I tried to listen to him, but what I saw when I looked down gave me such a shock that I didn't quite hear him. I saw that his sleeve had pulled up, and on his arm was a tattoo—numbers. I stared at it. You understand that we didn't know what it meant yet, but of course, now we know what it meant. I've seen many of those tattoos since then. But not enough. No, not enough."

"What do you mean, Grandma?"

"Each one that I actually get to see means another person who survived, and only a small number survived."

Debbie did not entirely understand, but she held her

questions. She saw her grandmother was deeply involved in her story. There was a faraway sound to her grandmother's voice, as if she was reliving this, as if she was there again.

"I stared at his arm. I couldn't help it. I was confused because the numbers scared me, but I didn't then know why. The rabbi saw what I was looking at and he said in a quiet voice, 'G-d has chosen us. For what reason, I don't know. I'll never know. But still, we're chosen. And we must not forget.'

"His voice was shaking," Grandma continued. "He bent toward me and said, 'You, my child, are going to America. You'll be an American! You'll forget about the old country. But that world is in you, no matter how far away you go. You can't escape it. You mustn't forget!'

"The rabbi turned away from me and went back to his books," Grandma said. "I picked myself up—the ship was pitching back and forth—and held my mother's candlesticks in one hand and my brother's hand in the other. The two of us left quietly and walked rather aimlessly out to the deck. We tried to talk about our future, but it seemed so new, so unknown. So we talked about our past."

At Grandma Eva's pause, Debbie asked, "What kind of tattoo was it?"

Shivering at the memory, Grandma Eva continued, "The tattoo was letters and numbers, which marked him as being in a prison camp. The Nazis killed the people in the prison camps. But they didn't get to kill everyone. The rabbi was a survivor. Maybe he escaped."

"Don't worry, Grandma," Debbie snuggled closer.

"I know, child. I know." She hugged her granddaughter.

Debbie couldn't speak. She tried to imagine herself at her own age and far from her family. She couldn't imagine being separated by a war and an ocean from her whole family and her home. *Imagine me turning twelve while I sailed toward a world that was so different! Like moving to Mars. I'd even miss Miri!*

Grandma Eva sighed. "I guess you really appreciate what you have when it's all taken away from you," Grandma Eva said, as if reading Debbie's mind.

"Oh, Grandma," Debbie said, putting her arms around her grandmother's neck. "I love you and so does everyone in our family. I love listening to your stories. But why are you still sad? In the end everyone made it to America! Your parents came back to you."

Grandma Eva sighed, "Devorah'leh, there's something you never knew."

Debbie straightened up, a worried expression spreading across her face as her grandmother spoke.

"Besides my brother, your Uncle Eli, may he rest in peace, there was another child in my family, a girl." Debbie couldn't believe what she was hearing. *How come I never heard? Why don't they ever talk about her? They always tell stories about Uncle Eli!*

"Grandma! You had a sister?"

Grandma Eva got up and went to the bookcase. She

pulled out an unfamiliar-looking photograph album and handed it to Debbie. The album was covered with blue flowers and was labeled in her grandmother's old-fashioned writing: Esther.

Responding to Debbie's quizzical look, Grandma Eva said, "My older sister." She looked down at Debbie with a kind eye. Debbie was completely surprised. Grandma sat down close to Debbie on the sofa and together they opened to the first page. Grandma Eva pointed at one of the pictures. There, in the grainy black-and-white photographs, was a curly-haired version of Grandma Eva. A smiling little girl stood behind a toddling brother and infant sister. They were all dressed in old-fashioned, formal, starched clothes.

There were more photographs of the girl. She always seemed to be laughing—while playing with the family's cow, serving the baby birthday cake, stiffly posed on the first day of school, or caught in a candid moment, reading a book.

Grandma Eva sighed. "She was beautiful—so full of life. Esther was six years older than I, and I never wanted her out of my sight. I sneaked into her bed at night. I cried every morning when she went to school and I was still too young to go. She was so much fun! She always had new ideas for games to play. She was like a second mother for Uncle Eli and me. We were never jealous of Esther. It seemed like none of her friends could be, either, even though she got the best grades in the class."

Grandma Eva turned the page of the album. Esther was older in these pictures. She was slimmer and her hair was braided and tightly wound into a bun. She wore a grown-up looking skirt and fitted jacket and shoes with a slight heel. She looked like a young woman. "I remember that outfit," Grandma Eva mused. "It was for her twelfth birthday. Esther looked so glamorous to me!" Grandma Eva let out a laugh. "She let me dress up in those shoes and I nearly fell."

The older woman held Debbie at arm's length, then she pulled her closer in a fond embrace. "You know, Debbie, you've always reminded me of her."

Debbie couldn't hold back any longer. "But, Grandma, where's Esther now?"

Her grandmother turned another page in the album. There, the teenage Esther posed with her family and some friends. She looked less carefree, more serious, and much older.

"This was wartime, Debbie. You can't imagine what it was like. All of a sudden families were slipping away in the middle of the night, never to be heard from again. The store shelves were so empty! All there was to eat was what we could grow in our garden. Mama did what she could to keep us fed, but we were hungry. The worst part was the rumors we'd hear about the concentration camps. At first no one believed the stories that went around, but we started realizing that there must be some truth to them. By that time, though, it was too late to get out. Papa applied for American visas, but we were told it was impossible for Jews to get them. We may have just been kids, Debbie, but like Papa used to say, 'There's no childhood in wartime.' We knew what was happening and it terrified the three of us—Esther, Eli, and me. Well… it terrified Uncle Eli and me."

Grandma Eva paused. "Esther was different. It seemed like she was always running off to some kind of meeting, always whispering with Mama and Papa when she thought Eli and I were asleep. I lay in my bed at night and listened to the hushed voices and wondered. I could hear the strain in their voices and the sound of it made my heart pound, although I did not know why. Then, one day, she was gone. I woke up in the room we shared and she just wasn't there. Her bed was neatly made, and laying on her pillow was a package with my name written across the top. Inside, I found this."

Grandma pulled her necklace out from under her sweater. It was a familiar piece of jewelry to Debbie, a small gold Jewish star. She couldn't remember ever seeing her Grandmother without it, but she'd never known it had such an important history.

"That's why I never take it off," Grandma Eva said, fingering the necklace. "In the package, Esther also left a note." She turned a page of the album. There, stuck beneath the plastic, was a yellowed sheet of paper inscribed in a perfectly round Yiddish script. Grandma Eva translated:

My dear sister,

I'm gone now, and someday you'll know just why. I wish I could stay. I wish I could tell you goodbye, or even kiss you as you sleep so sweetly curled up in your bed, but I can't. I can't wake you to explain. Perhaps we'll sit together as old ladies, eating Mama's cookies and talking about our grandchildren and knitting, and laugh about these crazy times. I hope so. But until we're together again, you must know how much I love you and miss you. I will think of you every day and pray to G-d to make us a family again soon, not just you and me and Eli and Mama and Papa, but all of us, all Jewish people. I pray to see you again in the land of milk and honey, a place of peace.

Grandma's voice broke. She blew her nose and continued:

Be a good girl, Eva. Help Mama and Papa. And always remember that I will find you again, in this world or in the next.

Your loving sister,

Esther

Debbie felt like her whole world was changing. She felt completely drawn to this girl. A deep sadness settled into her as if she had lost her own sister. Grandma Eva silently turned the page to the end of the album. The final photo was a close-up of two smiling girls, their almost identical pairs of eyes shining, their arms wrapped around each other. The inscription along the bottom of the picture read: Esther and Eva. Together forever.

Grandma Eva closed the album, got up from the couch and put it away. "Looks like it's lunch time, Devorah," she said. Her voice sounded cheery, but forced. "How about grilled cheese?"

"Grandma, how can you do this to me?" A wave of dread came over her as she guessed at the truth. "You can't just stop there. What happened?" she demanded. "Where's Esther?"

"I have some nice rye bread," Grandma Eva called from the kitchen. "I know just how you like it—with the cheese melted over a slice of tomato. And some pickles, right? Come to the kitchen and help me, okay?"

Debbie didn't respond. She sat motionless on the couch. She felt hypnotized by the big question mark that seemed to hang in the air. "Where is she, Grandma? Where is she?"

Grandma Eva slowly walked back into the room. She lowered her slight figure into a chair and leaned across the coffee table toward Debbie. At first Grandma Eva didn't speak, and then her face seemed to become more lined with wrinkles, the joy leaving her eyes. She sighed. "I never saw or heard from Esther again," she said quietly.

"What?!" Debbie gasped. "What do you mean? You had no word from her at all? How can that be?"

"Believe me, sweetheart, we tried. Your uncle and I and

your great-grandparents—may they all rest in peace—
tried everything we could think of. There used to be many
organizations that helped to trace missing relatives. Each
organization did the best they could for us," she sighed.
"We did find out that Esther ran off to join a resistance
group. Papa knew that too. He tried to discourage her, but
Esther was brave and determined. They were a loose band
of teenagers and adults who worked together secretly to
save as many Jews as they could. But anyone caught working for the resistance was shot. No questions asked. Papa
told us one day that he knew of the weapons that she was
smuggling to help the Jews fight the Nazis. But after we
escaped to France, we lost all contact with Esther. Later,
we found out that she became involved in another part of
the resistance that Papa knew nothing about. She helped
to smuggle children to safety in England. The work Esther
was involved in was the most dangerous kind; it had to be
highly secret because of the danger. No one in the resistance was to know what other workers were doing, so if
they were caught and tortured they wouldn't be forced to
give the Nazis any help catching more Jews."

Grandma Eva leaned back against the soft cushions of
her chair. "Esther was a heroine. I often wonder if I would
have had the courage to do what she did. I was too young
to understand what was going on, but Esther knew. She
knew that Jewish people had to be saved."

Debbie absently stroked the plush back of an embroi-
dered throw pillow. She couldn't believe it—she wasn't

sure what to think. Until an hour ago, she'd never even heard of Esther. Now, suddenly, she was related to this brave and tragic young woman.

Grandma Eva continued, "For years we put advertisements in newspapers around the world in hope of finding Esther, or at least someone who knew what happened to her. We hoped that after helping so many others, she had made it to freedom. We wanted her to know that we were safe, too. We went through the lists of the death-camp victims and searched through photographs." Grandma Eva shook her head slowly. "Finally, it must have been ten years ago, a few years before your grandfather died, we just gave up. There comes a point in time when you just have to give up. You have to say it is G-d's will and think about the good times. We try to remember Esther as we knew her and hope that she didn't suffer too much."

Grandma Eva looked into Debbie's eyes. "It's like what that rabbi on the ship told me on my Bat Mitzvah, Devorah. We can never forget. But we have to live our lives."

Debbie felt devastated. She felt like she had never been so sad in her life. Suddenly something occurred to her. "Grandma Eva, Miri and I are both named after other relatives who passed away before we were born, and I know that's a way of honoring them. So why aren't Miri or I named after Esther?"

Grandma Eva wearily rubbed her eyes. "I guess I couldn't face it, Devorah. Your mother asked me just after both you girls were born if I was ready, but I wasn't. We had given up the search, but I still couldn't face the truth. You are named after a cousin of mine who died in that ugly war. She was a beautiful young woman who went to her death as a proud Jew. I see that pride in you."

Grandma Eva crossed over to the couch and settled in next to Debbie. "But mostly what I see in you, Devorah'leh, is Esther. That same spark for life, that same brave intelligence. Thank G-d yours doesn't have to be tested like hers. But every time I see you, I'm reminded of my sister and it makes me wonder just how much she is guiding you from above."

She took Debbie's hands in her own. "Still, I can't give her up." Grandma Eva smiled sadly. "We stopped searching through the agencies, but I still keep Esther in my mind. Your late grandfather used to try so hard to get me to lay poor Esther to rest."

"So why... ?" Debbie asked, leaving the question unfinished.

Grandma Eva spoke so quietly that Debbie had to lean closer to hear. "Because maybe... maybe she's still alive somewhere."

CHAPTER EIGHT

For the next two days, Debbie could hardly pay attention in school. She thought constantly of brave Esther and her mysterious disappearance. In class, she often looked startled when the teacher called on her, and in the cafeteria, Leah almost gave up on her in annoyance at her silence. Debbie couldn't bring herself to be interested in the usual chatter. She was still quiet during their hurried walk to the next Bat Mitzvah Club meeting on Tuesday. They arrived fifteen minutes early.

When they walked into the room, Mrs. Levy gave them a big smile and pointed toward several grocery bags. "Go ahead and start setting up," she said. "I have a feeling you two know how to set up a lovely party. I have to finish preparing my notes. I'll be here if you have any questions."

Inside the bags they found plastic bags containing

cookies, chips, and candy. Leah ripped open a bag of chocolate chip cookies and popped one in her mouth. "Leah!" Debbie whispered. She was truly embarrassed. Mrs. Levy turned her head and smiled at the sight of Leah chewing on her treat. "Not bad," Leah said to Mrs. Levy. "Homemade?" Mrs. Levy nodded and went back to her notes. *Gosh! I don't think anything can make her mad!*

Together, while Leah's mouth was still full of the cookie, they pulled out a paper tablecloth and packages of rainbow-striped plates with matching napkins. Debbie began setting places at the desks, which had been pushed together to make a semicircle. After a few minutes, she noticed Leah opening another bag. "Leah!" she whispered again.

"What, Deb?" came Leah's reply, muffled through a mouthful of pretzels. "All this work's making me hungry." Debbie's face reddened.

"Hah!" Debbie quickly replied. "How about working off all of those treats? Let's arrange the food while there's still some to put out."

"Sure, Deb," Leah said, somewhat puzzled. "Sure." Together they finished the arrangements. Still, Debbie's doubts were starting again. *Why do I have to be embarrassed by my best friend?*

Ruthie Shapiro stood before the Bat Mitzvah Club, the fingers of her right hand drumming nervously on her notes, which she held in the crook of her left arm. She was a tall, athletic-looking girl with a graceful air.

"Welcome, everyone," she said with a broad smile. "I am today's Mistress of Ceremonies, but you can call me M.C."

"Okay, M.C.," someone called out. Everyone laughed.

Ruthie absentmindedly pulled the purple ponytail holder from her thick brown hair and slid it onto her wrist. "First of all," she said, consulting her notes, "Allison Levin would like to make a special presentation about giving tzedakah...or, charity."

Everyone clapped politely as Allison stepped to the front of the room, clutching her papers. Allison had curly red hair. Leah elbowed Debbie. "Gee," she whispered. "She really got dressed up for this." Leah pointed at her own scuffed tennis shoes with a wry grin.

"Hello," Allison said as she boldly looked out at everyone. She flashed a wide smile. Her silver braces shone.

"My job today," she said, "is to collect tzedakah from everyone. People say that tzedakah means charity, but I read that it really means 'right' or 'righteousness.' Charity sounds like a gift you give because you feel generous. But 'tzedakah' sounds like something you have to do, 'cause it's just right. So I'm going to call it tzedakah. I've always known that it is very important to give money to help people who need help, but I wanted to understand more about it. So... I asked Mrs. Levy..." A few people laughed. "...and I found out some things about tzedakah that I would like to share."

Allison held up a small tin box. "Everyone knows that it

feels good to help other people. But did you ever wonder why? What I found out is that the reason it feels good is because it's a mitzvah. We think that it's nice to slip a quarter or a dollar into a tzedakah box because later on someone who really needs it will get this money. Like, we decided it's the right thing to do. Right?"

"Right," all the girls answered back.

Allison then put her hand on her hip. "But, you know what? It's not really our decision to give. At all. It's our obligation. We're required. And that's the real reason we feel so good about it—it feels like it's up to us to give, like something important depends on our giving, like we're doing something we really should. So we do. And then we feel good, because what we're really doing is something that G-d says we have to."

Allison looked nervously around the room, as if her initial resolve was weakening. "Do I have it right, Mrs. Levy?"

"You're doing fine, Allison," Mrs. Levy said.

"My mother helped me, too," she said in a very small voice. There was laughter. She gave a small, nervous giggle herself, then she cleared her throat. "And another thing," she continued. "We might say that we can't afford to give it, but that's not true at all. Because the amount of money we decide to give to tzedakah was given to us by G-d for that reason. So that dollar isn't only in our purse so we can buy a soda or hairclips. The whole reason G-d makes sure it's there is for us to give part of it away and do a mitzvah.

"I'm going to pass around the tzedakah box. Please give whatever you can. In a few months, we will all vote to see what we would like to do with our Club's tzedakah. Thanks," she concluded with a smile.

One girl in the back of the room began to clap. Soon everyone was applauding. Debbie was impressed. Then a few girls began digging into pockets or backpacks or purses for loose change. *I wish I had my wallet with me. I'll have to remember on Tuesdays to bring more than just what I need for the cafeteria.*

Debbie watched Allison carefully as she passed the tzedakah box around. *I could do that. I thought you had to know so much to give a talk, but I could do one like that.*

Ruthie stood up again. "Thank you, Allison. Now, I would like to ask Michelle Fine to come up for our Heart to Heart talk."

Michelle looked nervous. She stood in front of everyone, but Debbie noticed that her hands shook slightly. She kept her eyes looking downward as she read from the papers she was clutching in her hands. "Good afternoon, everyone," she read in a quiet, shaky voice. She pushed her straight blond hair behind her ears and adjusted her glasses before continuing. "I would like to tell everyone a story. There was once a man who had a field and he never took care of it because he thought that the rain would fall and make his crops grow. When the rain did fall, though, the field was left the same as before. He looked over the gate and saw that the rain made his neighbor's crops grow. He didn't understand. So he went to his neighbor and asked: 'How can it be that the rain gave you such a beautiful field, but nothing happened to mine?' The neighbor answered, 'But there's more to it than that! You sat back and waited for the rain and did nothing. Every day I went out and prepared my field for the rain. I plowed, sowed, and fertilized. I worked hard. Then the rain did the rest.'" As Michelle read, the shakiness in her voice went away. Her voice grew stronger.

I'll bet her mother helped her do that, Debbie thought. *But Mrs. Levy doesn't seem to mind. And it's OK even to read it. I wonder if Mom would help me—I wouldn't know where to get a story. If Michelle can do it even when she's so nervous, I guess I could.*

Michelle looked up. "This story has a lesson," she said in a somewhat louder voice. Her shyness seemed to be going away, but she continued to read instead of using her own words. "It showed me that we can't just sit around and wait for things to work out. In order for G-d's blessings to work, we have to do our part first. And that means doing our best to do mitzvot. That's like preparing the field. Then we will grow up and be fine people. That's like the good crop that comes from G-d's blessings."

Everyone clapped as Michelle walked back to her seat.

"Thank you so much, Michelle," Ruthie said. "Now we will take our break."

During the break, Leah wanted to talk about The Dress and the swim team and a fight she'd had with her brother that morning. Debbie felt bad, but she did not really listen. She was thinking about Esther again and couldn't make herself interested in what Leah was talking about.

" ...and you won't believe what he did! He broke into my phone call saying he had some emergency call to make... "

Debbie fingered her journal, and picked up her pencil to write. *I've been feeling like I lost something and don't know where to look. I remember the time we went camping and Miri and I went hiking in a new part of the woods we hadn't explored yet...*

"I see you're really interested in my problems today," Leah said sarcastically as she licked the chocolate icing off a cupcake.

"Sorry, Leah," Debbie said. She really was sorry. *I don't like anyone to ignore me!* "Of course I'm interested. Maybe I'm just sort of thinking about some stuff."

"What kind of stuff?" Leah demanded.

"Oh, I don't know," Debbie replied. "I had a long talk with my grandmother on Sunday. We talked about her Bat Mitzvah. I guess that made me think a lot about my Bat Mitzvah."

"Debbie," Leah countered, "don't turn serious on me. Who'll I pass notes to if you start paying attention?"

"I know, Leah. But it's like I can't even help it. Sometimes we learn interesting stuff in school, but it's like, that's all it is. Stuff. Here we're learning all these things, but they're not just things—they're us. It's so neat."

"Neat, yeah," Leah said grumpily. She looked like she was about to say something else, but then Ruthie stood up and everyone quieted down. "Now I would like to introduce Amy Lieberman for a special presentation for all of our Bat Mitzvah girls."

Amy came up to the front with a long package cradled in her right arm. Her dark ringlets swung aside as she lifted it up to show everyone. "I would like to present a red rose to a club member who is celebrating her Bat Mitzvah birthday this week. First, though, I will explain why we are giving her a rose. The main reason is that everyone loves getting roses." All the girls laughed. "Another reason Mrs. Levy told me is that it's mentioned in the Torah that the Jewish people are like roses. Wherever we are, we blossom and flourish." *Nice.* Debbie smiled as she imagined herself stepping up in front of the group to receive her rose.

Amy consulted her notes. "So—a big mazel tov to Melissa."

Everyone clapped as Melissa got up from her seat. A camera flashed when Amy handed Melissa a rose. Debbie looked up to see Mrs. Levy smiling behind her camera. The flower was prettily arranged with baby's breath and wrapped in cellophane.

Amy cleared her throat and began to recite:

We all know Melissa is a great friend,

Anything you need, she'll always lend.
She works hard at whatever she tries,
And that's why Melissa has become so wise.

Ruthie stepped forward. Amy blushed and took an energetic bow to the loud applause from the class.

"And now, Mrs. Levy will speak to us for today's Bat Mitzvah lesson," Ruthie said.

"Uh oh," Leah whispered to her. "Here goes." Debbie said nothing, but smiled slyly to Leah as if she knew her secret. *Sometimes Leah pretends to be above it all when she's really interested. I saw how Leah listened at the last meeting, even though she'd never admit it.*

When Mrs. Levy stood up, she said, "I've got quite an act to follow. I must say I am impressed with the thought and hard work that was put into preparation for today's meeting."

"Watching Ruthie, Allison, Michelle, and Amy speak told me that I don't need to do all of the speaking. Watching them also gave me the idea that there are probably quite a few more of you who can help to run things. So I have an idea. But first, please get out your journals."

Mrs. Levy wrote a few words on the board. "I'd like you to write this down on the inside covers of your journals and really think about the words. Write a few lines about what you can do that shows this. Meanwhile, I need three girls to help me."

Mrs. Levy chose three girls. She gestured to them to

follow her out of the room and put her finger to her lips as if the four of them had a secret. Debbie smiled. Then she looked down at the words she had just written surrounded by the clean whiteness of the inside cover: "The mind rules over the heart." Her own heart began to pound. She didn't know what to write.

"Leah," she said to her friend. "I feel like this is a math test or something—and like I didn't study."

Leah looked at her quizzically. "Don't worry, Deb," she said. "Write the first thing that you think of. No big deal."

"What are you going to write?" Debbie whispered. She felt like she was cheating.

Leah looked thoughtful. "Heart means feelings here, right?"

"Yeah."

"So I guess I'm going to say it means that you have to think about what's right before you do something, even if you really, really feel like doing it."

Debbie looked at Leah with real respect. She let her jaw drop in mock surprise. She felt like she did when Leah knew the math perfectly and Debbie didn't get it. *How does she just… think of things when I can't get them?* She looked around her. Some girls were writing. Some were talking to each other. *Maybe they don't know what to write, either.* She chewed on the end of her pencil for a minute, and began to write.

"I think this means that feelings can't be the boss. But, all the time I hear people say to do something if it feels right, or to follow your heart. Is that bad?" Debbie didn't know what else to write, so she looked around at the other girls. She wasn't the only one who was finished.

Just then, Mrs. Levy came back in the room with the three girls. She was holding a shopping bag that looked like it was full of jumbled clothes. "Well," she said. "Did you decide what to write?"

Debbie's hand shot up. Mrs. Levy nodded at her questioningly. "I just wrote questions," she said.

"Have you heard of the Talmud? It is all Jewish learning, and it is full of questions! Questions can be a powerful way to learn." Her tone was reassuring. Debbie sighed.

"Feige, Erica and Sarah have a little skit to show you. The problem is, it's not finished and we're going to need you to help finish it. I'll give you one hint how to do this: The answer will be connected to the words I gave you just now to write in your journals."

The three girls were rummaging in the shopping bag. Feigie put on a wig that made her look like a lady. Erica didn't put on anything. Sara put on a shirt with lollipops in it, and then put her thumb in her mouth. Then the skit began.

Feigie was the mother. Erica was her teen-aged daughter, and Sarah (who was quite short anyway) played a small child. The three were at a large clothing store for a shopping trip. They pretended to be impressed with how big it was, and Erica pretended to hold different items up to herself to admire.

"Erica!" "Mommy" said. "You must hold your little sister's

hand so she doesn't get lost. My hands will be too full."
Together they walked through the store for a moment, and
then "Mommy" stopped to choose some items. They went
to pay. Erica began to act bored.

"This isn't fair," she thought out loud. "I want to shop,
too. Come on, Sarah. Mom! I'm going over there to look,
OK?" Mommy waved her hand in a distracted way. "OK,"
she called without looking back.

Erica walked away a few steps and pretended to see
something she loved. She dropped Sarah's hand and put
the "dress" up to her. "Ooooh, nice. Where's a mirror?"
She raced away from Sarah, and began to turn and dance
in front of the "mirror." Sarah made a big grin, and dashed
offstage.

"Erica? Erica!"

"Yes, Mommy. I'm over here," Erica said in a distracted
tone of voice without looking away from the mirror.

"And Sarah?"

"Sarah's here, too," she said. "Sarah? Sarah? OH NO.
WHERE'S SARAH?"

The three girls stepped out together. "Mommy" took off
her wig. *It's over? That's all?* Debbie thought.

Mrs. Levy stood up. "Where is Sarah?" she asked.
Several girls offered answers.

"She ran off."

"She crawled under a rack and she's hiding."

"She's looking for her mother."

"Why did this happen?" Mrs. Levy asked.

There was quiet for a moment. Many hands went up. Amy spoke first. "Well, Erica should have been watching her sister, but she wanted to look at the dresses."

Mrs. Levy smiled. That twinkle in her eye came back when she said, "But, maybe it wasn't fair to Erica. Maybe she needed some shopping time, too!" Everyone started to speak at once. "Now, hold on so you can be heard," Mrs. Levy called. The girls settled down and spoke one at a time.

"I think it wasn't fair to Erica. Sometimes big sisters have to be like mothers, so the mothers can have a good time."

"I don't agree. If her mother was nice, Erica could ask if she could look some, too, without having to hold her sister's hand."

"Maybe she could ask if they could get a baby-sitter next time and go out together; just the two of them."

"I have a little sister like that and sometimes she's a real pest."

"So maybe," Mrs. Levy asked, "maybe it was OK just to let Sarah run off?"

"Nooo," everyone said, laughing.

"Why?"

Debbie's hand went up. "Because... because she's a sister. Because we have to take care of our families the most. I mean, I don't mean if she was somebody else's sister that Erica could just let her go, of course. But... because she's family, well, Sarah was even more her responsibility."

"So now what should she do?" Mrs. Levy asked.

"She has to find her. She can't stop until she finds her." Debbie thought of her grandmother and felt sad for a moment. *What happens when you look and look and you can't find your own sister?*

Mrs. Levy looked up at everyone. "What does this have to do with what you wrote in your journals while you were waiting?"

Leah's hand shot up. "That's simple," she said. "Her heart wanted to feel good trying on dresses. But she was supposed to think first. Her head had to tell her, 'Not now. Talk to your Mom and make a way you can get what you want next time.'"

Debbie thought about looking at dresses in the Unique Boutique. *Great, Leah. Think first. But your head thinks of the craziest things!* She laughed.

"The thing to remember," said Mrs. Levy, "is that G-d gave us a *yetzer hara*, a natural desire to indulge our feelings without thinking. But you have to direct traffic between what your heart wants and what your mind knows. Your parents have really been responsible to guide that. But after Bat Mitzvah, you are supposed to hold that responsibility first, before your parents have to step in."

There was a chorus of "Oh, no!" from the class.

"Don't panic," Mrs. Levy said reassuringly. "We all make mistakes—that's part of growing. The key is to try our best—start practicing to think before we act. Now's the time to start training yourself to check in with your mind before you go along with your heart. That's the best

Bat Mitzvah preparation you can do."

"Here's a trick," she said. "When your feelings, what you really want, don't fit with what your mind tells you is a better choice, like when you'd rather watch television than study for math, even though you know better..." Debbie winced. "Just imagine how good it feels to really be in control. And imagine the good outcome—understanding what's going on in class." She smiled and picked up her papers. "We'll talk about this more next time. Have a great week. See you next Tuesday."

The class laughed and began to gather jackets and backpacks.

"You know, Debbie?" Leah said. "I could do without this responsibility stuff. Couldn't we skip growing up?"

"Sure," Debbie said with a grin. "Got a quarter?"

"Here. Why?"

"I'll just call and let your Mom know you're going back on baby food."

Leah laughed. "Mashed bananas were always my favorite."

"And," Debbie added, choking with laughter and the effort of getting the words out while she laughed. "Your bedtime's going back to seven o'clock, OK?"

"Thanks, friend." Leah said, laughing, and playfully punched her arm. Then she pulled up short. "Oh no, swim practice!"

The two quickly gathered their things and ran out the door.

Later, Debbie and Leah were walking home together after swim practice. Debbie shivered slightly in the cooler air at the end of the day, especially since her hair was still wet. Houses and trees made long shadows. The horizon was streaked with orange. Debbie loved how she felt after swim practice—cool, energetic and relaxed. And she loved walking home with Leah afterward, chatting and laughing all the way. She felt generous. She decided to share her secret about Esther with Leah.

"Leah, guess what."

"Well, it's about time you told me what. You've had something cooking in there all week. Is it about your grandmother?"

"How'd you guess?!!"

"You said you'd been thinking about something since you went to your grandmother's house and she told you about her Bat Mitzvah. I didn't exactly have to guess."

"Leah, she had a sister. Can you believe it? All my life, and I didn't know my grandmother ever had a sister. She ran off before they left Europe to escape the Holocaust. She wanted to join a secret group of people who were trying to save Jews… and no one ever heard from her again!"

"She died?"

"If she did, no one knows. My grandmother told me how she kept looking for her sister for years and then gave up. I just keep thinking about her. I saw pictures. My grandmother says I'm like her."

Leah stopped still in her tracks. "Debbie, come here. Stand up straight." Debbie did so in mock obedience. "Now!" Leah announced to an invisible audience. "Announcing Debbie! The fabulous freedom fighter!" Debbie giggled and took an exaggerated bow until her head almost touched her knees.

Leah's face grew serious. "Debbie, I don't get it. You mean they gave up looking for her sister?"

"Yes," Debbie said. "They tried everything, and didn't know where else to go."

"Well?"

"Well, what?"

"Don't you want some ideas how to find her?" Leah had a playful look on her face and a big grin.

Debbie loved these games with Leah. She could see the wheels of imagination spinning away in Leah's amazing head. Together, no matter how old they got, they could pretend anything. She giggled. "Sure," she said.

"All you have to do, see, is find out about a group going to Europe for a convention or something. You have to make friends with one person going, and zip yourself into their suitcase. When you get there, you just start interviewing people and... you'll find Esther in no time."

Debbie was crouching down. She held up her hands as if they were against something hard and flat right next to her. "Help!" she shouted. "Help me! My zipper's stuck!" They were both laughing. Debbie fell over backwards onto the grass. She looked up at Leah.

"I wish I could find her, but I wouldn't know how. Anyway, so many grown ups have really tried. What could I do that they can't?"

Leah pulled her up and patted her arm. "We could figure out something," she said. "I'll bet we could."

For the next few weeks, Grandma Eva's story stayed in Debbie's thoughts. She couldn't concentrate on anything—not school, shopping with Leah, even swim team. She went to practices, and Mrs. Brown pushed her harder than ever. She even went to several extra practices that her father urged her to schedule with Mrs. Brown as well. It was nice of Mrs. Brown to take the extra time for her, but she knew she wasn't concentrating like she used to.

At home, she wandered around her house like a ghost. Debbie didn't even protest when Miri borrowed her cashmere cardigan without asking. "I'm just lucky I have a sister," she told herself when she caught Miri sneaking the sweater back into Debbie's room.

Miri really looked surprised that Debbie wasn't angry. But she couldn't come up with even a hint of what Debbie's problem could be. Finally, Miri asked her mother.

Mrs. Solomon smiled and smoothed Miri's hair. "She's growing up, Miri. You'll see when you get to be Debbie's age."

Debbie devoured the stories she read of Holocaust victims and survivors, especially girls like Anne Frank, who was close to Debbie's own age. She closed her eyes and tried to recreate the feelings from a dream she had. She saw herself as she was in the dream, sewing big yellow stars onto her coats and sweaters. Sometimes she paused and stared through her window and down over fences at children walking to school, children who were still care-free, playing in the parks now prohibited to her. She could nearly hear that dreaded knock on the door in the middle of the night. Her heart sped up at this sign that the Nazi storm troopers had found her family's hiding place.

Debbie read about the Jewish partisans and tried to imagine Esther among them, meeting in the deep of the forest, whispering code words, passing along plans to blow up Nazi convoys, leading people on long, treacherous journeys to the free world. She imagined Esther, brave Esther, cold and hungry and scared, but always full of spirit, filled with hope.

Debbie looked around her at her comfortable room—the warm bed, soft carpet, the closet full of clothes. *How could I possibly think of what it's like to be Esther? I've always had everything!* She sighed and her eyes fell on her Bat Mitzvah Club journal on her desk. She gathered it and a pen, and flopped down on her bed to write.

"Sometimes I pretend that I'm Esther and I've run away from home to rescue Jews," she wrote. "Grandma Eva says I look like her. I wish I wish I wish I knew how to find Esther!"

CHAPTER NINE

et's talk about Bat Mitzvah," Mrs. Levy said, writing the words in large letters on a blackboard in front of their semicircle of desks. "What does this mean?" Debbie looked at the words.

"It's what happens on our twelfth birthday," Amy said. Amy was one of the members that Debbie knew from school. Her birthday was just before the cutoff date, and Debbie's was just after, so Amy was in the next grade ahead of her.

Mrs. Levy had that mischievous look about her again. Leah leaned over to Debbie. "What does she have up her sleeve?" she asked.

"Break it down," Mrs. Levy said. "What's the first word?"

"'Bat' means 'daughter of'." It was Ruthie speaking.

Debbie knew her from the Jewish Community Center. Debbie looked around the room. She liked the way that the desks were pulled into a semicircle, and the way that she didn't feel like she was in a classroom. *I feel like we're just all sitting around talking to each other*. She felt comfortable there now, and knew everyone.

"Why do you think 'Bat' is part of what happens to you when you turn twelve?"

Debbie spoke up. "Maybe it's connected to what happens when we turn twelve... to our Jewish soul, and the way we have to do our own... mitzvot now," she said hesitantly.

Mrs. Levy smiled at her. "This word here means 'daughter of...' and not just daughter, yes? It's a word we use to say she's connected to someone. Who are you connected to? Who do you come from?"

"My parents."

Mrs. Levy drew a double circle on the board.

"And they? Who is your mother the daughter of?"

Mrs. Levy drew another double circle overlapping with the first, like links in a chain.

"Her parents."

With each question she added to the chain on the board. Now Debbie was sure that's what she was drawing.

"And them?"

"Their parents."

"Back into history?"

"Yes."

"So… are we linked to our history?" Mrs. Levy enunciated each word with force, as if she couldn't possibly ask anything more important. Debbie looked up, startled. Many of the girls nodded yes. Mrs. Levy turned and drew one last link on the chain on the board. "Come here," she said. "Everyone."

The girls all stood up and shyly stepped in front of their desks.

"We all know each other by now, no? Show me how you would form a chain." Someone laughed. Hannah boldly stepped up and offered her two arms forward, forming a circle, and invited someone to make the next link. Another girl came, and another, each one linking her rounded arms into the previous one. Soon they were all linked into a human chain. Mrs. Levy joined in with her arms linked through Leah's.

"We are daughters of our history and of our people," Mrs. Levy said while the girls stayed in their formation. "That is the 'Bat' part of 'Bat Mitzvah.' And what connects all of us, what makes us Jews, is the 'Mitzvah' part of 'Bat Mitzvah.' Follow the mitzvot from the Torah and you will always feel that true Jewishness, and you will always stay connected. The strength of the chain depends on its links. Keep your link strong!" She looked at them. When they finally broke up the chain, somehow Debbie didn't really want to let go.

Debbie thought about Esther, and about people like the Germans who tried to destroy her and break the chain.

She had never thought about the past being connected to her. She felt close to Esther and to all the people who were persecuted. Somehow she felt that, by doing mitzvot, she was helping them.

"Well, what does a chain do?" Mrs. Levy was asking when Debbie tuned back in.

"It holds things together." Melissa had the answer.

"Say it in one word," Mrs. Levy urged.

Melissa thought hard. "It... connects," she said.

"Good!" Mrs. Levy answered. "What does a mitzvah connect us to?"

Debbie had the answer. "To history. To Jewish people who have come before us and wanted to do the same mitzvot," she said.

"The chain of history," Mrs. Levy said. "A powerful connection. Perhaps we can complete the mitzvot that others were prevented from doing. What else does a mitzvah connect us to?"

Again there was silence.

"Who else does a mitzvah connect us to?"

Who else besides all of the Jewish people? Debbie thought. She was embarrassed at her hesitation.

"When your father asks you to do something, and you do it, do you feel a special connection to him?"

Debbie smiled. *G-d asked us to do them. I get it!* Just then someone came out with her answer.

"G-d."

"Yes!" said Mrs. Levy. We forge a link with our people.

We form a link with our history. We stay connected to G-d. That's really three chains, isn't it?" Debbie imagined herself holding the end of a three-part chain that stretched endlessly back on the path behind her, far into her past.

CHAPTER TEN

eah tugged at her arm. "Gosh, Deb. Did you go into a trance, or what? Don't forget we have the junior finals meet at 6:30."

"Oh, wow!" Debbie exclaimed, jumping to her feet. "Let's go," she said. The two girls hurried out the door.

Debbie didn't feel ready for any meet, let alone such a major event. "I haven't been training as hard lately," she told Leah. "I don't know, I'm not so into swimming these days."

"I can't believe I'm hearing this," Leah said, as the girls rushed along the street leading to the Jewish Community Center. "You can't let the team down!" Leah paused and looked like she was thinking for a moment. "Team? The whole city's counting on you," she said to Debbie with a smile. The Jewish Community Center was in a league that included swim teams from around the state. There were teams coming in from other cities for this competition.

"Besides," Leah said in a mildly mocking tone, "Jewish girls have to be good and perfect and responsible all the time."

"You know, Deb," she added. "I don't know if I like all this Bat Mitzvah stuff. I'm just in it for the presents."

"Yeah, right!" Debbie said, ribbing Leah. "I saw how you were listening at the last meeting." Her voice changed to a more serious tone. "They talk about Jewish pride. Don't you wish... don't you wish you could use all this stuff we're learning to do something really big and brave like... " Her voice trailed off.

"Like?"

"Like Esther did?"

"I'll take my safe, comfortable life, thanks," Leah said. Her voice was muffled because her mouth was full of pretzels she had brought from the Club meeting. She offered some to Debbie.

"Thanks," Debbie said. "I forgot to eat and I'm starved. I guess we won't get another chance until after the meet."

The girls rounded the corner and ran from there to the building and inside to the locker room full of their chattering teammates. All of a sudden, Debbie was nervous. Really nervous. *I just haven't had my mind on my training lately, in spite of all the time I've spent practicing. It's as if I wasn't really there.* Debbie thought about the talk she had with Mrs. Brown.

Last week, Mrs. Brown must have noticed that she was distracted, because she called Debbie into her office for a conference. She wanted to know if Debbie was having problems at school or at home. Debbie assured her that everything was fine, it was just that she had a lot of school-work. She promised to get her mind back on her swim-ming. She wanted to. She really did.

I really want to concentrate on doing well. I'll just tune my Jewish soul into being the best junior freestyle swim-mer in the state. I can do it. Mrs. Brown said I'm one of the top three in this event. Again, thoughts of Esther intruded. *She did much, much harder things than this....*

And here she was, in the middle of her giggling, excit-ed teammates, feeling alone.

For the first time ever, Rachel Levine came over to Debbie before the race to shake hands. "I hope the best swimmer wins," she said.

"Thanks, Rachel. Let's swim a good race today," Debbie replied as she shook Rachel's hand enthusiastically.

"You can bet on that," Rachel said, and suddenly sur-prised her with a knowing grin. Then she saw her coach and quickly moved away to her team's side of the pool area.

Debbie scanned the room. The place was quite large. Usually their local swim-meets only filled a small part of the stands. Today, all the stands were filled. Just then Debbie found her mother among the sea of faces. There they were! She caught Miri's eye and they waved at each other. "Good luck," her mother mouthed, waving at her.

I'll need it, Debbie thought. *Luck. I still haven't topped the time I made when I tied with Rachel Levine earlier in the season...*

Debbie felt a pull at her elbow. "Debbie, what are you doing? Dreaming?" Mrs. Brown called. "You're up next!"

Debbie didn't have time to think. The time had arrived! She walked with Mrs. Brown over to her starting position. Her heart was pounding, although she paid little attention. It seemed as if everything else was far away and the whole world consisted of Debbie and the pool in front of her. Her breath came quickly. She was ready. At that moment, she wanted to prove something to herself. She wanted to tackle this challenge more than anything in the world. She adjusted her goggles and stepped into position, then looked to her left and to her right at the girls at the head of each lane, waiting for the gun.

"Debbie, I know you'll do your best," Mrs. Brown said. "You always do when it counts. And doing your very best is just the same as winning!" Mrs. Brown smiled up at the young girl. "You've got it in you, Debbie. Remember that." Debbie felt a chill run through her.

Suddenly, it was just Debbie. Lined up on either side of her were the other racers, with Rachel Levine, deep in concentration, on her left. Debbie stared into the still water. Her eyes traveled the distance of her lane. The water was so clear. It looked like air. It seemed as if she could sprout wings and fly across and back. She looked up at the stands. *Wow.* The crowd was large and silent. Waiting.

Debbie's heart pounded.

"Bang!" The starter pistol erupted and Debbie gasped in a breath. With all of her might, she took off and hit the water. *Great start!* She glided to the surface, her legs madly kicking.

Debbie's muscles strained as she pulled through the water. She flipped through her first turn so smoothly that she surprised herself. *I'm flying!* She marveled, fixing her mind on the image of herself with wings. Meanwhile, her arms and legs ached with effort. Debbie sped through the race, not even daring to check on Rachel's progress. *I'm doing my best.* She gulped in air before her final turn. *I'm doing my best!*

It was the straightaway to the finish line—the final push. Debbie made her arms and legs work even harder. Her feet smacked the water so quickly they felt like a powerful motor. Her arms reached farther, harder, faster. *Go, go, go, go!!! This is it!*

Her muscles felt like they would explode. *More, more, more! I won't give in to the pain!* Debbie told herself this as she sped up even more. Then, she was there.

She forcefully slapped the end of her lane and sank back into the water. Her heart pounded. *I won't look yet.* Her arms and legs hurt so much. She shook away the pain while her limbs were still underwater. *I know I did my best.*

Debbie couldn't stand the suspense. She snatched off her goggles and pulled herself up at the edge of the pool.

She heard a deafening sound. Wild cheering. She glanced over to Rachel's lane. There was her closest competitor with her head hung in defeat. *Couldn't be,* Debbie thought as she turned to look at the scoreboard.

"**YOU DID IT!!!!**" Leah shrieked from the water's edge. Confused, Debbie turned to face the crowd. "Me?" she asked in disbelief. Then she saw her teammates jumping with excitement. Before she knew what was happening, Debbie felt herself being pulled out of the water. She was still dripping wet, as her cheering teammates hoisted her onto their shoulders.

Debbie whooped with delight. The spectators all seemed to be shouting her name. She found her mother and Miri in the throng, shouting and dancing with joy.

Her teammates finally let Debbie down, and Mrs. Brown covered her with a towel. Debbie had never seen her coach smile so broadly.

"You've got it in you, Debbie," Mrs. Brown shouted above the din. "You're a winner!"

Debbie made her way over to Rachel, who sat dejectedly on a bench at the pool's edge. She held out her hand. Rachel managed a smile. "Congratulations, champ!" Rachel said. "Great race!"

"Uh, thanks," Debbie replied. She was impressed that Rachel could be such a good sport. "Are you okay? You don't sound too good."

"I feel lousy," Rachel said. Her voice was very raspy. "I got a cold. I can't breathe."

"Sorry to hear that," Debbie offered. "Say, maybe we could get together sometime. Go jogging or something," she suggested.

Rachel's face lit up. "That would be nice," she said. She smiled. "Enjoy your win, Debbie. There's nothing else in the world like it."

Debbie looked at the spectators perched in the grandstands. There were her mother and Miri trying to catch her eye. She waved. She looked at the scoreboard, which still posted the results of the last event. Her event.

There was her name: D. Solomon. And her position: Number One. And there, beneath her name was R. Levine - 2.

Debbie looked at the last column of the scoreboard. She looked at her time and her jaw dropped. It couldn't be, but it was true. She had won, but her time was nearly four seconds slower than it was early in the season when she tied with Rachel. She looked down the column at Rachel's time. Debbie couldn't believe it. Rachel's time was nearly a second slower than hers.

Oh, I haven't done anything! I haven't done anything at all. I thought I was doing so well. What have I accomplished? Nothing. I didn't win! Rachel lost. She had a cold and she couldn't breathe. She probably belongs in bed instead of in a swimming pool. But what's my excuse? I did the best that I could, and it was still four seconds slower than my best time. Rachel was sick. What's my excuse? Debbie started to cry.

Debbie was still crying when Leah and Mrs. Brown

came over to her. At first they thought that Debbie was crying tears of joy. But then Debbie managed to get out to them all that she had just been thinking. Even Leah, no matter how good she was at being a clown, couldn't put a dent in Debbie's resolve that she had failed.

Mrs. Brown held Debbie by the shoulders and close to her broad chest. "Leave us, Leah," Mrs. Brown said. "Go watch the next race with your friends." Leah did as she was told and managed a meek wave at Debbie. Mrs. Brown told her assistant coach to handle the next events and then she led Debbie to the locker rooms.

When they got there, Debbie lost control again. "But I don't deserve any credit. Not one bit!" she managed to get out between her sobs. "I didn't win. Rachel lost!"

"Debbie, stop that talk right now," Mrs. Brown commanded. "You won."

Debbie tried to interrupt, but Mrs. Brown held up her hand and said, "You be quiet for a moment and let me talk." Debbie's sobs subsided a little, and Mrs. Brown began: "Now I know you didn't have the best time you ever had, and I know Rachel didn't either, but you won the race. And that came with each one of you doing your best. You put in one hundred percent. Rachel gave one hundred percent. Each one of those girls out there gave it everything she had."

She sat down on the bench next to Debbie before continuing: "You girls always talk about how you should have given one-hundred-ten or one-hundred-twenty or one-hundred-fifty percent. Where do you get such ideas? You can only do the best that you can on any given day. If you give all that you've got of yourself to give today, then that's one hundred percent. Period. And that's all that anyone, including yourself, can expect of you—I don't care if we're talking about swimming or music or algebra. All I want you to do is to look inside yourself and say, 'Coach, I gave it one hundred percent and this is the best that I could do.' The winning or losing part will sort itself out. Even if you come in first it doesn't always make you a winner. And if you come in second it doesn't make you a loser. Not in my book. And winning is an attitude. You have to show that you're a winner before you can be treated like one."

Debbie stopped staring at the floor when Mrs. Brown ended her speech. She looked up and faltered at first before saying in a firmer voice, "I did do my best."

Mrs. Brown held Debbie's shoulders and raised her to her feet. Then she bent her knees in order to look directly into Debbie's eyes. "In that case," she said, "you're a winner!"

CHAPTER ELEVEN

Debbie had made up her mind. Everything sort of came together at the same time—the Bat Mitzvah Club; Esther; her swimming victory; and now—her English teacher's latest assignment. Mrs. Brown's talk after her last swimming race kept ringing in her ears. *I'll give it my best, even if I don't succeed. I can't even know if I have a chance to succeed if I don't try.*

The English assignment sparked her idea. Mr. Hankins looked positively gleeful when he stood up in front of the room. Debbie looked at him. His faded shirtsleeves were rolled up above his elbows, and an undershirt peeked out at an open collar. His thinning hair was slicked back and there was a pencil behind one ear. Debbie had to smile as if she noticed his customary combination of dress pants and tennis shoes for the first time. *I wonder what he's got planned.* "Let's see everyone get involved in something new," Mr. Hankins said as he moved his gaze across the room. He smiled and gripped his palms together in front of him. "Your assignment is like this: Come up with a new idea, an invention, a plan, or a problem to solve. Then research it."

About ten hands went up in the room. There was a buzz of excitement. Some students looked genuinely puzzled. A few seemed upset.

"Mr. Hankins, I don't understand!"

"Can we get help?"

"Does this have to be pretend, or real?"

One girl folded her arms with a scowl. "I'm not an inventor! How do you expect me to do something like this?!" Several others made faces as well.

"Why can't it be about another subject, like science or math?"

"What if somebody else gets the same idea?"

"What if you think of the problem, but you can't solve it?"

"How long does this paper have to be, anyway?"

Mr. Hankins chuckled. "Hold on. Hold on!" he said. "Let's not all speak at once!" Slowly he answered their questions, one at a time. He gave examples that students had used in previous years, but emphasized that they could not be copied. "I know such an unclear assignment can make some of you nervous. But we will always encounter new ideas that have to be explored or new problems that need a new kind of solution. This is an important skill to practice. I don't even care if what you try turns out to be impossible," he said. "I want to see all of you do your best—even if it doesn't mean coming in first," he added with a smile toward Debbie. *He must have heard about my swimming! I'll bet they all talk in the teacher's lounge.*

"It's the process I'm interested in," he continued. "Your reading and research. And, of course, your written report. Write down your plan, and I want to see evidence that you really thought about the problem. I'll help you get started," Mr. Hankins said. "We'll talk about how you are going to go about doing your research." Just then the bell rang. "I want to speak with each one of you individually before the end of the week. I'll post a sign-up sheet on my door," he called as the class filed out for the next period.

Right away Debbie knew what she had to do. She was thinking of Esther. Sometimes she lay awake at night and imagined how Esther would lie awake at night the very same way, probably thinking of how she could help the Jewish people.

That night, after dinner, Debbie went straight to her room and flopped down on her bed with her Club journal. "I've got to use my Jewish soul to make the world a better place," she wrote. "That's what Mrs. Levy would say. Maybe not in a big, impressive way. Maybe just in my own way."

"I want to find Esther," Mr. Hankins read aloud at their

conference the next day. "Or, at least, find out what happened to her." He turned to Debbie, who was nervously twisting her hands in her lap, and adjusted the small, round glasses on his nose. "I'm not sure I've ever seen such an original research paper idea," he said.

Debbie smiled with relief.

"But," he said forcefully. "This is a big project you're proposing. You've only got until the middle of April to do what your grandmother's been struggling to do for fifty years. What makes you think you can do it?"

Debbie's mouth felt dry. She drew up her courage. "Mr. Hankins, didn't you say it was OK if we don't succeed? How will I know if I can or not? I... I just have to try," she replied haltingly.

Mr. Hankins smiled a broad smile. He seemed happy that she had answered as she did. "Even if you end up right back where you started?"

Debbie nodded. She felt as if she was being tested. She was losing her fear. She felt as if she was passing the first part of the test.

"Debbie, you could be setting yourself up for a big disappointment. You're a bright girl, but you're facing a fifty-year-old mystery that professionals couldn't crack. You have to be realistic. The odds that you'll turn up anything new, much less locate your great-aunt, are small. It has only been a day since I gave out the assignment. Are you sure you've given this enough thought?"

"You... you said in class that it's the work we do that

counts, not the results," Debbie said again. She felt shy, but somehow she managed to look up to meet Mr. Hankins's eyes. "I want to try."

Mr. Hankins nodded and sat back in his chair. After thinking for a minute, he said, "Okay, this is what I want you to do. Think seriously about this, and how you'll go about your research. Then, over the weekend, sit down and discuss the project with your parents. I don't want to cause trouble for encouraging you to dip into something that may be a sensitive issue in your family. You want to open a book that your family may believe should be kept closed. If they think you should go ahead, then we'll get together to make a plan for how you'll start tackling your research."

Debbie gulped and let out a meek "OK," but inside she was celebrating. *Yes!! I get to do it!* She smiled weakly at Mr. Hankins, meeting his eyes, then looked briefly down at her shoes and grinned. She looked up to find him smiling warmly back at her, and there was a twinkle in his eyes. She gathered her books to leave.

"And Debbie?"

"Yes?" She looked up from her books.

"Good luck!"

Debbie's smile was broader now. *He really meant that. I'm gonna need it.* "Thanks! Thanks a bunch!" she said, and, hoisting her books, she left the room.

Out in the hallway, Leah waited impatiently. "I demand that you tell me exactly what's going on, Debbie!" Leah's hands were planted firmly on her hips. "You haven't been yourself for weeks, and I'm getting tired of having a space cadet for a best friend. If I am still your best friend. I mean, maybe you've replaced me with Rachel Levine," she added in a mocking tone. "Come on. You know I'm good at keeping secrets."

Debbie giggled and looked away from Leah's intent gaze. *Sure you are, Leah!*

"Well," Leah sighed and then conceded, "I could always turn over a new leaf and become good at keeping secrets!" After a pause, she added, "I'm pretty sure I could, anyway."

Debbie started down the hallway toward the cafeteria, Leah in tow. "I really don't mind telling you, Leah. And it's not like I've been keeping a secret. It's just that… did you ever want to keep something to yourself because you didn't want other people kidding you about it or shrugging you off? And… maybe I need to keep quiet some more so I can… picture it in my mind. Like when you try something on for size to make sure it fits just right."

"What are you talking about? I don't get it," Leah interrupted. She stopped still in the hallway. Someone almost bumped into her. She looked unusually serious. "Anyway," she said slowly. "You're right, Deb, it might take a while for me to deal with it, but… I'll get over this eventually. Really I will."

Debbie laughed. "Now I don't get it. Get over what?"

"Your parents are getting you the dress."

"What!? What dress?" Debbie asked, genuinely puzzled.

Suddenly it dawned on her. "Oh, The Dress?"

Leah nodded with the same serious expression and Debbie laughed out loud. "Oh, Leah, I forgot all about that dress! No way! I wouldn't take it away from you! It's exactly perfect for you!"

Leah let out a sigh of relief. "Oh, good! Yes! You know we couldn't both wear the same dress. And guess what? I think I have my parents convinced. What shoes do you think go best? Plain black pumps?"

"Yeah, sure Leah. Sure. You'll look great!" Debbie replied. She was happy for Leah. She suddenly felt real warmth for her friend. Right then and there Debbie decided to tell Leah her plan. "Leah," she said slowly, as she hooked her arm in her friend's arm and directed her on down the hallway toward the cafeteria. "It's not that I have such a big secret, but I'd rather other people didn't know all about it yet."

"Yeah... " Leah said with a grin, bending her ear toward her friend as they walked. "I'm all ears!"

"Remember the story about my grandmother's sister Esther?" Debbie said in a low voice.

"And will you ever let me forget it? I've been fighting her for your attention since you first went to your grandmother's house!"

"Leah, I've decided what to do."

"You're going to do it! You're going to Europe!"

They both laughed. Debbie almost doubled over. Instead, she bent her knees and put her hands up again as if she was stuck in a suitcase.

"Help!" she said.

"My... zipper!" they both said together, and then collapsed in laughter.

"Really, Leah," Debbie said, holding her side and trying to make a straight face. "I mean it. I'm going to do it. To.. try and find her."

Leah looked so pleased she didn't even crack a joke about the cardboard-like veggieburger or mushy peas that the cafeteria lady was sure to heap on their trays. Together they proceeded to the cafeteria to collect what was passing for food that day. They both gravitated toward two seats alone, away from their regular group, and bent toward one another to speak quietly. Debbie looked up to see Jennifer waving at her and pointing to an empty seat at their table. She looked at Leah. Leah noticed Jennifer, too, but smiled and waved back as if she was saying "hello." She turned back to Debbie.

"Wow, Deb. I mean, your poor grandmother, spending all those years hoping Esther will come back. She knows better, I'm sure. I mean, wasn't she just pretending to herself that she'd see her sister again?"

"Maybe not," Debbie said slowly.

Leah saw a look of determination on her friend's face. Debbie usually got this look just before a race. "Debs, you can't be serious."

But Debbie was serious. "I have to try," she said in measured tones. Then she outlined for Leah her conversation with Mr. Hankins.

Leah, too, picked out the obvious questions. "Deb, what makes you think you'll turn up anything that all these adults haven't found? How will you feel if you find out something bad? How will your grandmother feel? Maybe it's better not to know."

"I thought about that. But, Leah, don't you see I have to try?"

"Maybe Mrs. Levy will have some ideas for you," Leah offered. "Maybe ask her at today's Club meeting. She might know about some group that keeps track of tracing family roots, or something like that."

"That's a neat idea. Oh, look," Debbie said, waving at the clock. The girls jumped up and pulled on their backpacks. Then they got rid of their garbage and hurried to Mrs. Katz's math class and quickly took their seats. They were late.

"By the way," Leah whispered to her just as Mrs. Katz turned around to write an equation on the board. "Don't tell your parents. I don't think they'd exactly understand." Mrs. Katz turned around and glared at them. Leah promptly turned back to her workbook.

CHAPTER TWELVE

ebbie was sitting next to Leah waiting for the Club meeting to begin, thinking about the events of the day. She knew the teacher said to discuss her project with her parents, but she did not want to tell them about it at all. Debbie thought Leah was right. *I'll have to keep this whole thing a secret. They'll worry too much and take the project away. They'll tell me to pick something else that doesn't have anything to do with us. For sure they'll think it's too hard, or that it might upset Grandma.* Debbie usually got high grades in English, and her parents trusted her to keep up with papers and homework without reporting her activities in that class to them. *Lucky they don't follow Mr. Hankins' class so closely. But what, oh what, do I tell Mr. Hankins when he asks?* She tried not to think about it, but planning a secret made her nervous. She felt like she was lying.

Debbie also agreed with Leah about asking Mrs. Levy. There was something in the way Mrs. Levy taught that made Debbie feel like more than just a kid. *It's like she respects every one of us in the Club. And it doesn't matter if we're gorgeous or smart or anything. It's something else—an appreciation for the real person on the inside. Maybe Mrs. Levy can really see our souls. Maybe she has X-ray vision. I'm going to try that.* The M.C. introduced Mrs. Levy's portion of the Club, but Debbie didn't notice. She was writing in her journal: "I'm going to try to think about people's souls instead of just seeing the way they look on the outside."

Mrs. Levy pulled up a chair in front of the semicircle of chairs. "Let's talk," she said. "I have just one or two questions for you, and I want to hear your answers." She was quiet. She looked and waited. The buzz of talk in the room stopped. Everyone was looking at her expectantly.

"Let's pretend that a new Club member showed up today that you have never met. Naturally, you take a good look at her when she first arrives. What gives you some clues about her personality?"

Allison spoke right out. *She's never shy. Even when her braces make her talk funny.* "I'd look at the way she walked in," Allison said.

"What do you mean?" Mrs. Levy was interested.

"Well... did she seem scared, or... what."

"If she was, how would she walk?"

"Slowly. Maybe with her head down."

"So the way a person carries herself talks?"

"Sort of." Alison shook her red curls. She smiled at Mrs. Levy.

Mrs. Levy turned to the rest of the group.

"What else? Michelle?" *Michelle won't speak up on her own. But I like to hear her.*

Michelle was quiet and thoughtful for a moment. Mrs. Levy waited and did not fill the silence.

"I think... I think I'd look at her face, and especially her eyes."

"How so? What could her expression tell you?"

"Well, it could tell me... if she really wants to be here or not."

"So maybe she's smiling and looking excited?"

"Or maybe her parents made her come and she's missing going swimming," Leah said ruefully. Everyone laughed. Debbie did, too.

"OK," Mrs. Levy said to everyone. "A person's facial expression says something about her, too. That's two things. One: how a person carries herself, and two: the attitude that shows on her face. Does everyone agree?"

Debbie raised her hand. "Well... it says something about her right then, but not always."

"It tells us something about her present mood?"

"Yes."

"Does a first impression make us decide more about her? Does it possibly make us think she's always like that?"

Many of the girls nodded.

"Is she? Is she always like that?" Voices erupted.

"Yes."

"No!"

"Maybe."

"So first impressions can affect our thinking?"

"Yes!"

"Even though they are sometimes incorrect?"

Silence. Then a number of heads nodded.

"What else tells us something about our new, mysterious Club member?"

Melissa answered. "I'd look at how she's dressed." The girls began making comments to each other. Everyone wanted to talk. Some laughed, but to Debbie it sounded like they laughed because they would look at a new girl's clothes, too, like Melissa said. *Me too, but I'm glad Melissa said it. I wouldn't.*

Mrs. Levy smiled. Debbie could tell she really liked Melissa's answer. Mrs. Levy put her finger to her chin in a thoughtful manner, and asked, "Well... if the girl's clothes could talk, what would they say?"

Silence.

"I'll tell you what," Mrs. Levy said. "Take out your journals. Take five minutes to write your best answer. Pretend to yourself that the girl's clothes are really speaking to you, and write down what they say. Then we'll talk."

Some of the girls groaned. "But, Mrs. Levy—I don't know what to write."

Mrs. Levy just smiled. "I'm not grading you," she said.

Debbie sat thinking. She looked at Leah, who was already busily at work. *But I'm not like Leah. I hardly notice what people are wearing. What if clothes don't talk to me at all? I really don't notice, unless...* Suddenly she got an idea, and started to write. She was thinking about her Bat Mitzvah. She was thinking about The Dress, and about Leah.

The five minutes were up, but Debbie kept writing. She knew Mrs. Levy wouldn't interrupt her. Mrs. Levy spoke to those who were finished. "Would anyone like to share what they wrote with us? Amy?"

Amy's dark curls shone. She cleared her throat. "The new girl's clothes tell me something about myself, because I compare myself to her. I think, 'Do I look like her? Do I look as nice, or nicer?'"

"Amy, you confirm my faith in this class," Mrs. Levy. "I'm always touched by how deep you girls can be. You see, you can do the teaching." Amy beamed.

The girls continued. Gradually the picture grew. Everyone agreed with Amy—that when they look at how someone else is dressed, it makes them check out their own appearance. All agreed that the clothes "tell" them about the girl's personality—bright or somber, her cleanliness, her neatness, and whether she likes herself or not. "So," Mrs. Levy asked the group. "What kind of clothes would you want to choose for yourself?" Everyone began talking at once. "Ruthi?" Ruthi's thick brown hair was not in its customary ponytail. She shook it out of her face before she spoke.

"Good-looking ones," Ruthi said, and laughed. Plenty of the others did, too.

"Our Jewish souls are a part of G-d. We call G-d our King. So what does that make us? Daughters of a King! Should your outside reflect that?" Mrs. Levy paused. Slowly, more and more of the girls nodded their agreement. Some hands went up.

"Sometimes people dress in a wild way to get attention."

"I think they want to be something they are not," said Mrs. Levy. "But we know what we are."

"Most people don't care. They just want to dress any way they want."

"They don't know what you know: On the inside we are all daughters of a King. But be careful!" Mrs. Levy added with a twinkle in her eye. "Remember what we said about how a person carries herself and her attitude. If you dress like a princess... you'll have to act like one!"

Debbie thought about The Dress. The Dress was all wrong for her—the color, the style. Everything. It was too grown-up looking. On her it would shout. But it blended nicely with Leah's shape, style, and coloring. Leah had worn other things in a similar style. On Leah it would not "speak" so loudly.

Then Mrs. Levy asked Debbie to read.

Debbie swallowed hard. She felt her face become red,

but she forced herself to go ahead. She glanced at Leah, who made a funny face that brought a nervous giggle out of Debbie. "This is why you get The Dress," she whispered to Leah. Then she cleared her throat.

"I'm not so sure clothes really talk at all, or if they should. I usually don't notice what people are wearing, unless what they are wearing doesn't fit them right, or if it's loud or the wrong color for them or not clean, or wrinkled or too short. Maybe the best clothes are the ones that are not these things, so that you only notice the person's face and attitude. Maybe clothes should keep quiet."

Leah was looking at her. Debbie leaned over and whispered. "I get it now. The Dress would be all wrong for me, Leah, but it compliments you." Leah beamed at her.

"I love it!" Mrs. Levy said. "Debbie, you really understand why modest clothing is the mark of royalty. I wouldn't have thought of your words. That's why there's a whole group of Jewish rules about how we dress—so we'll dress just right for a princess!" Just then, Debbie felt like one.

CHAPTER THIRTEEN

Mrs. Levy didn't lift her eyes from Debbie's face while Debbie told Esther's story. Debbie held tightly to Mrs. Levy's attentive gaze and returned the look so intently that she saw herself reflected in Mrs. Levy's eyes and began to feel as if she was talking to herself. Debbie was nervous as she spoke, but she recounted everything, from the tiny Polish village to Debbie's English classroom just last week. When Debbie finished, she heard her last words echo in the quietness of the classroom. For a moment, there was total silence.

Debbie smiled tentatively at Mrs. Levy. Her teacher looked so serious. *Maybe she doesn't like this whole thing. Oh no! Then who will help me?*

Finally, Mrs. Levy cleared her throat. "I can try to help you, Debbie," she said. Debbie let out an audible sigh of relief. The teacher took a sheet of paper and wrote down some names. "These are some agencies that you can call. I don't even know how much these searches are done any more. After all these years, many of the survivors have picked up the pieces, married, lived their lives, passed away, and their children rarely keep up the old ties. Sometimes, the children don't even know the old family names." She tapped her fingers on the desk. "You've picked quite a task for yourself. But I'll tell you, I'd do the same in your place."

"I know you would," Debbie said shyly. "That's why I came to you for help. You talk all about the importance of our souls and of being Jewish women. I feel like, I don't know, like I can't really know who I am until I find out about Esther."

Debbie read the teacher's next question from the look in Mrs. Levy's eyes. " ...even if the news isn't good," she added.

"Debbie, I'm rooting for you, and not just because I want you to find out about Esther. I think that whatever happens, you're going to find out much more about yourself."

After swim practice the next afternoon, Debbie raced to the library. There, she had her first taste of the difficulties that were ahead of her. After explaining her assignment to the librarian, Debbie followed her to the stacks, where she was shown a couple of reference books: a book of government agencies and one of associations.

Debbie pored through the pages of the book on government agencies. She didn't really understand the purpose of all of them. From what she could tell, the only agency that could give her any help was the Bureau of Immigration, but the librarian said that they could help only if Esther had come to the United States. *No way. From Grandma Eva's story, she just couldn't have made it here.* One down, one to go. She turned back to the book of associations. It was really five books—four books and an index.

The index contained alphabetical listings of all kinds of organizations. The listings were broken down by category. From the size of the book, it seemed like there was a group for everyone who had a cause. There were professional organizations for dentists and taxidermists, for epidemiologists *(whatever they are)* and cosmetologists. You could find people trying to clean up the environment listed alongside people trying to pollute it. *This shouldn't be too hard. All I have to do is come up with a list of key words and I can find my group, too.*

She looked in the index under "Missing Persons" and found a few associations that looked promising. *I can't tell if they search locally, nationally, or worldwide. And do they only search for people who disappeared recently? What if their searches stretch back more than fifty years?!* She sighed, and then copied names, addresses, and phone numbers into her notebook. She turned the pages of the index.

There were nearly fifteen hundred entries for Europe and three hundred for Poland. Debbie read through the fine print until her eyes were tired and her mind was numb. Then she took a short break and read some more, always keeping her goal in mind: to find Esther. She looked at the huge book. *I'm not going to give up. I won't.*

She finished both categories and thumbed through the book to World War II. After she read through a few of them, she realized that her key words were too general. *I have to be more exact or this will take weeks. Maybe I'll look under the word "Jewish." There ought to be a lot of Jewish organizations that could help me.* She thumbed through the pages and found the category: it had about four hundred entries. *This looks more like it. I can see some possibilities already.*

One category that looked promising at first turned out to be all wrong. It contained dozens of listings, but they were not for her purposes. Then she found a group that provided information on war victims. She read further— "FOR MEMBERS ONLY." *Too bad. I have no money to pay membership dues. Still, I'll write the name and address down anyway. Maybe they'll help out a girl who's trying to find a family member all by herself.*

Debbie copied the information from a few more listings into her notebook. She looked at her watch. *I better get out of here or I'll miss supper. At least I made a start. The sooner I get this part done, the sooner I can start writing letters and making phone calls.*

Debbie returned on Thursday after spending two previous afternoons at the library. The entries under the headings "Holocaust" and "Human Rights" were filled with the kind of information she was looking for. *This is a job for the copy machine.* But when she found the machine, it didn't make change. Then, when she got change, the copies came out so blurred that she couldn't read them. *Oh well. It's writer's cramp time.* She sighed and turned back to her pen and notebook.

Finally the list was as complete as Debbie could make it and Debbie decided she'd done enough research. After that, she began rushing home from school each day to make phone calls.

Debbie called the local organizations first, but most of the groups on her list were either in New York City or Washington, D.C. There were also a few in Philadelphia and Baltimore. That meant that most of the offices she was contacting were not in her time zone. *Chicago's time is one hour earlier. I hope at least some people will still be in their offices when I call after school. I have to speak to a real person and not an answering machine. What if I leave a message and someone calls when Mom and Dad are home? What in the world will I tell them?*

I'm just not going to worry about long distance calls. Daddy has to call New York all the time for his business. If I keep the calls short, they probably won't even notice a few more calls to New York. And maybe, maybe they won't notice a few short calls to the other cities, either. I'll just have to take that chance.

Every agency she called transferred her from department to department. More than once she was transferred back to a person she had already spoken with. No one knew exactly how to help her out.

"What? You want what?" asked one elderly man wearily. "You want to find someone no one heard from for how many years? Don't we all."

After many frustrating calls, a nice woman at one of the agencies took the time to listen to her.

"Honey, why don't you call the Holocaust Museum in Washington, D.C.? I'll bet they know someone who can help you. Here—I'll give you the number. Got a pencil? I wish you luck…"

Debbie called there immediately.

"Holocaust Museum." The receptionist's voice was cool and professional.

"Hello. Um… I'm, um, looking for someone who can help me look for a relative who… disappeared… during the Holocaust." She finished the sentence in a rush, relieved to have gotten it out.

"You need the Survival Registry. One moment please." Debbie couldn't believe her luck. She waited impatiently for someone to answer her ring. *Oh, I hope, I hope they can help me!*

"Survival Registry."

Debbie repeated her request for help in finding Esther.

"Well..." The man sounded hesitant. "You have to understand that we have only sifted through a small portion of the information that the museum has received from the time of the Holocaust. It has been possible to trace Holocaust survivors and reunite them with their families in a few cases. I have seen it. The Nazis kept amazingly careful records about all of their victims: Lists of deportation trains, lists of people on the trains, people on work details, people put to death in the camps, and the "causes" of death. We've also got lists of people who inquired about getting out of Europe, and registration lists from many cities and towns. The museum has been going through these records. We're working with the American Red Cross to identify any information that can be useful in tracing victims. The Red Cross is working with an international tracing service. Since the Iron Curtain in Russia and Eastern Europe came down, a lot more information has become available to the relief agencies, so that's good for you. And a lot of this information is now on computer."

Computer? Yes! Then it's so simple. I'll just ask them to do a search on their computer.

"But there are some real problems with that kind of search." Debbie's face fell. "A search will take quite a bit of time. We've got access to nearly forty-six million documents from all over Europe telling us about nearly fourteen million people. But even though we've got lots of names, ages, birth dates, and occupations, a lot of this information is just not accurate. People lied. They lied to survive. They said they were younger than their age so they would be put to work instead of killed. They claimed useful professions if they had none. They denied being Jewish. Anything to escape the terrible punishments that were inflicted first on the elderly and unskilled. All of this the Nazis dutifully wrote down. That's what we've got." The man's voice turned cold. "Lists and lists peppered with lies."

Debbie couldn't speak. She wanted to cry. *How am I ever going to find Esther? Grandma Eva couldn't find her. Why did I think I could? What do I do now?* She held the phone mutely against her ear. She wanted to hang up.

"We can do your search," the man was saying. Debbie couldn't believe her ears.

"You will?" She asked meekly.

"We can do it, but don't count on us finding your… aunt is it? Now you have to do a few things first. You have to put your request in writing and send it to me. Write down everything that you can possibly tell us about Esther. Can you send a photograph? You don't have one you can send me? That's OK—just describe what she looked like and where she was last seen. It's going to be eight to ten weeks, but someone on the staff will contact you with the results."

"Thank you. I… I'll be waiting."

"No promises. But you will be contacted." She heard an

unceremonious click on the line and the man was gone.

"Eight to ten weeks," Debbie moaned after she hung up. "My report has to be finished before then!"

Debbie sat at her scheduled conference with Mr. Hankins on Monday. She was scared. Mr. Hankins was sitting at his desk going over test papers when she came in. He was holding the pencil that was usually perched behind one ear. He looked pleased when he finally noticed her standing just inside of the doorway clutching a sheaf of papers with her notes from the library.

"Debbie, how nice to see you. Please come in and sit down. This reminds me that I was going to call your parents and I was delayed. I want to speak with them about your project—I'm doing that for all the students. Would tonight be a good time?"

Debbie was desperate. "Tonight's really not good for them," she blurted out. "Meetings," she muttered, then dropped her pen on the floor and bent down to pick it up. When she straightened up, she couldn't avoid Mr. Hankins's eyes.

His look was concerned and direct. "You have told them, right?"

Debbie didn't know what to say. *If Mom and Dad find out they'll make me drop the project. But if Mr. Hankins finds out I didn't tell them, he'll make me drop the project.*

Mr. Hankins looked at her. There was a long pause. He

didn't blink. She did. "Debbie, this isn't a joke. It is obvious to me that this is too sensitive for you to even approach with your parents, but I thought you understood how important it is to have their permission. So, you can start another project on something that doesn't involve your family's personal matters. Of course, you'll start off more than a week behind the rest of the class, but I think you can complete another topic in time."

Debbie felt miserable. "I... I've already begun my research. I've spent so much time at the library." She took a deep breath. "I can't stop now!"

"What about your parents?"

Debbie breathed a shaky sigh. "Okay, I'll tell them." She looked at her teacher, and then at her lap. Her face felt hot. "Really, I will," she said softly.

"Debbie, can I trust you this time?" She nodded miserably and fought back tears. "Okay," he relented, "I'll wait until tomorrow night to call your parents so you can tell them about your project first. Let them know that I plan to call."

Debbie felt a tiny bit relieved; at least this meeting was ending. She brushed at her eyes, then gathered her papers and stuffed them into her backpack. "Thanks, Mr. Hankins," she said very quietly as she got up to leave. "Thanks." Her voice shook. She bit her lip to keep from crying as she turned away.

"Debbie," Mr. Hankins said gently. "We'll go one step at a time."

Debbie rushed home that evening. Inside, she was still quivering. *What if they forbid the project? I couldn't stand being left with unanswered questions about Esther all my life! How could I go on from day to day, wondering if Esther is still living someplace, wondering if she has a family that knows what happened to her? Maybe we have cousins someplace in Poland, or in Russia, or in Europe. If we could find them and ask… Maybe Esther died doing something heroic. At least I could find out the details and help Grandma Eva rest easier.*

I can't just switch to another project and leave Esther lost in the past!

CHAPTER FOURTEEN

"What!?" Miri exclaimed with a sour look as she stood in the doorway between the dining room and the kitchen.

"You heard right," Debbie said. She was just slipping the meatloaf into the oven. "Mom met Dad at work and the two went straight to some dinner party."

"And we're left at home with old meatloaf? Not fair!" Miri brightened up. "Debbie… maybe I'll see what Elise is having for dinner."

Usually, Debbie would prefer even Miri's company to being left alone in the house at night. Sometimes the two ended up having a great time making cookies or popcorn and playing games. But tonight Debbie relished the chance for some good, peaceful thinking time. "Sure, go ahead," she said as Miri dialed Elise's number. "Just make sure you get home by 8:30 or I'll get in trouble. Mom says their dinner party won't last very late."

As soon as the front door slammed behind Miri, Debbie turned off the oven and searched through the refrigerator for something more exciting to eat. *Why should I be left with day-old meatloaf on top of all of my problems when everyone else is out having fun?* She got out a large bowl and filled it with vanilla fudge ice cream. Then she added chocolate sauce, walnuts, and whipped cream. She took a bite, then stopped and added a sliced banana. *Fruit makes anything more healthy, right?* Debbie smiled and settled down at the kitchen table to devour her concoction. Miri would kick herself if she knew what she was missing!

Then Debbie thought of Esther. *What did she eat in the frozen Polish forests? Maybe some dried-out bread. Or a potato that she dug up and ate raw. She couldn't cook it—a campfire would give away her hiding place. Then she probably climbed under a pile of dirty blankets and went to sleep hungry.* Debbie imagined herself shivering under the blankets, pushing away thoughts of her mother's warm soups and soft, fresh bread. She looked guiltily at her nearly empty ice cream dish. *What Esther wouldn't have given for leftover meatloaf. Even cold.*

Debbie washed her dishes and headed to her room. *Oh, well. I might as well get some math problems out of the way while I wait for Mom and Dad to come home.*

Debbie had just drifted off to sleep over her math

homework when Miri pushed open Debbie's door. Debbie glanced at her clock. It was 9:30. "Forget your watch, Miri?"

"Sorry. We got involved in something," Miri said shyly.

They heard the front door open and close. "Don't tell Mom and Dad, okay? PLEASE?" Miri whispered.

Debbie looked at her little sister. *I've got to connect with her soul, and not the outside annoying part.* She made herself smile. "Don't worry. But next time, you better call."

"You feeling okay?" Miri asked with amazement. "I thought for sure you'd tell on me and I'd get yelled at."

"But Miri," Debbie said in a sugary voice. "You're my favorite little sister."

"I'm your only sister!"

"I'm just lucky to have you, that's all," Debbie said. She sounded sincere this time. *After all, didn't Grandma Eva lose her sister?* She looked at Miri and made herself smile. "You know, my new sweater would look great on you."

Miri reached over and put her hand on Debbie's forehead. "You don't seem feverish," she said. Debbie pushed her hand away and then tickled her. Miri jumped back laughing and tried to get her back, but Debbie's longer arms kept her just out of reach. Just when Miri let out a squeal of delight, their parents poked their heads into Debbie's room. Debbie's smile instantly dropped off her face. *Oh no. I'm gonna have to talk to them.*

"You girls having fun?" asked their mother. "You left

the kitchen awfully clean. And you left all that meatloaf. Guess that's what happens when we go out for a fancy banquet and leave you with leftovers."

"I'm still recovering from that fancy banquet," said their father, rubbing his stomach.

Debbie took a deep breath. *I have to do it. I have to tell them.* "Mom and Dad, I… " She got stuck.

"What is it, Debbie?"

"I have to talk to you tonight. It's important," she said in a rush. Her mother glanced at her father, and then back at her.

"Okay. Just give us a few minutes to change. I have to get out of these heels." Debbie's mother sounded mystified. She looked at Debbie curiously, then headed to her room.

Twenty minutes later, Debbie sat with her parents around the kitchen table. She outlined her project and watched her parents' expressions grow more and more worried. *It doesn't look good.* A definite frown was appearing on her father's face. Debbie nervously finished her speech and looked down at her folded hands.

After a few tense moments of silence, her mother began, "I don't know what to say. I'm so disappointed that you felt you had to hide everything from us." She really looked hurt. A wave of guilt swept through Debbie.

"But I understand why you did it," her father continued.

"You do?!" Debbie said with relief.

"Yes," her father said slowly. "I understand why you hid this from us, but that doesn't mean I think it was a good idea. As for the project—this could upset your grand-mother." *But Daddy! Grandma won't be upset. I want to do this for her!*

"The truth is," her father went on, "I'd like you to think about switching topics. We spent years looking. Your grandmother lost a lot of sleep, and it took her a long, long time to leave it behind her. And anyway, how in the world could you expect to fit this into a few short weeks?"

Her father sighed. Her mother nodded. "We'll think about it, Debbie, and give you an answer tomorrow evening."

Debbie sadly kissed her parents good night. Then she turned and walked out of the kitchen and trod wearily up the stairs to her room. She took her Club journal from her desk and settled into her customary position on her stom-ach on the bed. She began to write:

This is the worst possible thing. The worst possible thing of all. If my parents say no, and they sure look like they will, I'm finished. How could I ever leave Esther like that? The man at the museum said the odds are stacked millions to one against finding Esther, but how could I stop the search now and never know? I have to find a way to keep on going. I have to know what happened to her even if... even if.

CHAPTER FIFTEEN

Debbie's heart was just beginning to pound. She focused her eyes as best as she could on the bouncing image of the pavement in front of her and the repeated appearance of her running shoes alternating on the street. *Breathe. Slowly. Don't slow down. Breathe.* She glanced at Rachel's figure jogging beside her, one step ahead, her agile limbs easily moving down the lane. *I'll bet she's not even sweating.* Wordlessly, Debbie pointed to the neighborhood park on the corner, and the two headed to a bench when they reached the end of the block. The early morning sun streaked the sky with orange and the park bench was still wet with dew.

"We've still got some time, but I want to get back in time to shower before school."

"This is neat. You want to do this again tomorrow?"

"Maybe. It was hard enough to get my mother to agree this time. I don't know why—all we've done is run the streets right near my house in broad daylight." Debbie pictured her mother's worried face as she left through the kitchen door, and remembered how her mother appeared in the kitchen just when Debbie did so early in the morning. "She worries too much. I wish she'd just sleep in."

"Mine did. She probably still doesn't know where I am."

"Will she be upset?"

Rachel sighed. "No, probably not. She's got her mind on… other things."

Debbie's wish that her own mother would sleep late disappeared like a balloon that suddenly popped. She tried to imagine her mother not there in the morning, fussing over her, thinking of her, undistracted by "other things."

"Do you have sisters or brothers? Where do you live?"

"I live in the apartments at Tenth and Applethwaite. It's just me and my mom and my brother. My dad… split."

"Oh, wow," Debbie said involuntarily, and looked away, afraid she had made Rachel feel like a monkey on display at the zoo. She tried to imagine their belongings stuffed into one of those apartments. She was familiar with the apartments at Tenth and Applethwaite. They were nothing like the homey, spacious quarters where Grandma Eva had an apartment, even if the neighborhood wasn't as good as it used to be. Then she tried to imagine life without Dad, and could not.

"It's OK," Rachel said, as if she needed to console

Debbie. "You should have heard them before he left. It's better this way. Still, I miss him."

Debbie's heart ached. "Don't you get to see him?" she cried.

"Oh, sure. Sometimes. But he doesn't always make it over to see us when he says he's coming. And when he does, it's not as if we live together. He takes me places and buys me things. But I just want to see his face when I eat my breakfast."

"Does your mom work?"

"Yeah. Mom's really great, but she gets so tired from her job. I make dinner a lot. Richie—he's my brother—he's not much of a cook. Still, we get along, usually. And," she smiled, "I have swimming."

"You love it."

"I do. Nothing else matters when I'm in the water. It's so easy and cool. No sweat." She grinned and wiped her glistening forehead.

"You make it look so easy. And I think it's so hard."

"Did I say easy? I was wrong. I mean, I work hard. My coach works me hard. But it's fun work. I wish I could swim forever."

"That's the difference between us," Debbie said. "I tackle swimming, like it's a hard job. And you look forward to it, like some kind of..."

"Relief," Rachel filled in.

Relief. What do I need relief from? Not school, except maybe math. Not home. Maybe from Miri, sometimes.

And sometimes... Leah. But not usually.

"I think... I think swimming just isn't the same for me that it is for you." She looked at Rachel, and realized something. *I don't want it to be. I don't want to need it like you.* Debbie didn't need swimming in the same way and she realized she was glad of it. She felt suddenly safe, comfortable.

"Have you had your Bat Mitzvah yet?"

"Yes... and no."

"Wait a minute. What's the "yes" part and what's the "no" part?"

"Well, my birthday passed, and my mother still says we're going to do something to celebrate it, but..."

Oh no. Debbie felt embarrassed about all the fuss and preparation her mother was finally starting. *I have to say something.*

"I... I've been going to this Club," she blurted out, "and, maybe you want to come? It's called The Bat Mitzvah Club." *Oh, no. Now Leah's going to kill me. If Rachel comes I'll have to sit with her and Leah will absolutely pop.*

"You see," she continued, "even if you didn't have a party for your Bat Mitzvah, you still become something. You're still a Bat Mitzvah. That's what the Club's about. Besides... it's fun."

Rachel looked touched. "I think I'd like that. I'll try it." *Just like that—and she doesn't have to ask her mother! She seems like a twelve-year-old adult. She must feel as if*

she's on her own and in charge of her own life. Awesome.
Debbie glanced down at her watch somewhat nervously.

"Hey! Shower time!" The two jumped up and resumed their pace, this time more together, steady, jogging back towards Debbie's home. Debbie paced silently, and Rachel did not disturb her thoughts. "Call me tonight!" Debbie called, as she turned up the walk to her home without breaking stride. They waved at each other and she continued on up the walk.

Debbie came running into the kitchen, and completely to her mother's surprise, threw her arms around Mrs. Solomon in a bear hug. Without explanation, she broke her grasp and ran into the family area and up the stairs, singing. On the landing at the top of the stairs she whirled around and stopped, looked over the view of her mother's immaculate, well-furnished den and dining room, gave a large and generous smile, and turned toward the bathroom at the end of the hall. She just felt glad. She was glad to have her mother and father in the same house. She was glad to live in their calm, spacious home, and glad that her mother had time to worry about her. This was the first time in the Solomon house that Debbie was heard to sing in the shower.

CHAPTER SIXTEEN

It was settled.

"I don't know what finally clinched it," Leah said as she and Debbie walked home after Bat Mitzvah Club. "I think it was just that my parents were adding together all the costs of my Bat Mitzvah party and," Leah laughed, "the money for the dress and shoes didn't seem to matter so much next to the total bill. I didn't even have to trick them about the cost," she added with a smile.

"I'm happy for you," Debbie said, realizing that she really was happy for her friend. *I'm sure Mom's going to want to get me something really pretty for my Bat Mitzvah, too. It doesn't have to cost as much as The Dress. My whole Bat Mitzvah's not going to be as elaborate as Leah's. And I want it that way. No complaints.*

"Picture this!" Debbie said, laughingly elbowing Leah.

She held up her hands to dramatically illustrate her words. She tried to make her voice sound like the announcer on her favorite mystery show.

"First—a huge, decorated ballroom filled with elegant young women each dressed more gorgeously than the last, laughing and flitting from table to table." Debbie held her chin high in an exaggerated pose, and imitated the walk of a proud young woman in a long gown, her feet gliding along the floor.

"And the banquet! It's a mile-long table loaded with the fanciest food money can buy, around a ten-foot ice sculpture and… and a waterfall! And looking down over it all on a diamond studded throne…" Debbie moved Leah over beside the imaginary banquet table, "Princess Leah herself!" In awe at the spectacle, Debbie took a large step backward and made a deep and formal bow. "Of course, she outshines everyone else: She's wearing The Dress with perfectly matching shoes. The whole world is jealous." She winked.

Leah was laughing. She held up her imaginary scepter and said, "You may be seated." Debbie laughed with her, and sat down on the ground.

"Well," Leah said. "My Bat Mitzvah isn't quite like that, even if we do have the hall and The Dress and the ice sculpture. But no waterfall." She extended her hand to help Debbie up.

"No waterfall," Debbie said. "Me neither."

"Oh, Debbie. I'm embarrassed."

"Don't, Leah. I mean, I want my Bat Mitzvah to be smaller. You're the party girl. Not me." But just then Debbie imagined her own party. There sat her family and a friend or two dressed in everyday school outfits, sitting in the living room of her house, eating take-out pizza. Cold. From the box.

Debbie felt a little deflated. "We haven't talked about my party yet. Maybe my parents don't even want one. But that's OK, I guess." Her voice trailed off, sounding wistful. "We keep learning how important our Bat Mitzvah is, but…"

"But nothing!" Leah interrupted. "Don't be so silly, Deb. I know your parents. You're going to have a beautiful party. Mine will be gigantic and crowded and fancy and… too much. Yours will be perfect: friendly and, well, more personal."

That's what I like about you, Leah. Sometimes you know exactly how I feel even if I don't say. She pictured her family sitting around the kitchen table, all dressed in pajamas, crunching corn flakes. "I hope not too personal," she giggled.

"You know what I mean," Leah said. "Now don't get all jealous because my family likes to spend lots of money on parties and things. Remember my brother's Bar Mitzvah? He still hasn't recovered."

"Oooh. Remember the eyes on that salmon platter?" They both erupted in giggles. "Remember how quiet and serious your brother was?" she continued. "So many people kept crowding around him that he almost forgot his speech!"

They chatted some more about Leah's Bat Mitzvah until it was time for them to head their separate ways home.

"Call me tonight if you want to go over the math homework," Leah called to Debbie.

"I will!" Debbie called back.

As she walked home, Debbie thought about how different Rachel and Leah were. She thought it was good to have two such different friends. Then her thoughts turned back to Leah. *Phew! Good thing Rachel's name didn't come up during our walk. The other times I mentioned maybe going to the movies with Rachel, Leah got angry. She's acting more and more jealous. How come being with Rachel hurts Leah's feelings?*

Leah just doesn't understand. I have a different kind of fun with Rachel. Rachel can't replace Leah. I can't laugh as much with her. She's more serious, but I like the good talks we have. Still, I'd better tell my family not to tell Leah where I am if she calls while I'm out with Rachel. Rachel's so strong! I thought it was just in her swimming, but she has strong ideas about grown-up things, like politics. She's so interesting, even if I don't always agree with her! Leah makes me laugh and Rachel makes me think.

The sky was dim and streaked with pink lines as the setting sun shone through the clouds. Debbie stopped at the turn to her street and looked around at the bare tree branches reaching toward the gray, winter sky like arms flung straight up to heaven. Debbie tried to imagine what

Mrs. Levy would say about the scene. *Trying to touch G-d. Trying to connect, that's what we humans do. But we're not even as smart as a tree. Trees know what they're supposed to do and how they're supposed to do it. They don't go around trying to look like movie stars or get money or toys or clothes or fancy cars.*

G-d doesn't want me to be anything but me. Debbie smiled to herself, then frowned slightly. *So what's that?*

Debbie shuffled her feet as she turned onto the sidewalk leading to the front door of her house. She opened the door and quickly closed it behind her to keep the chill out. She took off her coat and hung it up. "Mom? Mom! I'm home!"

She went into the living room and climbed into her favorite overstuffed easy chair with big arms and soft cushions. She still remembered how her parents wanted to send it to the basement when she was five, and how she threw a fit over it. So her parents fixed the springs on the chair and put on new upholstery. *Daddy always sat here with me when I was a baby. I must have fallen asleep in his arms so many times.* The cushioned arms swallowed her up; safe and secure.

She leaned back in the chair and looked out the living room window, back at the path she had just followed. The front step, the sidewalk, the street. She thought of the walk home with Leah. The Club meeting. The last few weeks. She jumped up and ran to get her Club journal, then settled back into the chair's soft warmth and began to write:

"I want to know everything G-d wants me to do in my

life. It's too hard to decide on my own! Sometimes I feel bad about Leah's gigantic party. I just have to remember what's right for me. G-d wants Leah to honor her parents. They mean well. They just don't always do things the way Leah likes—even her own Bat Mitzvah. But Leah still honors them, just like G-d says. Still, I'm lucky..."

As she wrote these words on the page, she realized that she really was lucky. Debbie looked through the open door into the kitchen. She saw her parents preparing dinner. Miri was sitting at the kitchen table, reading her homework out loud to her mother.

"My parents look out for me. They told me this morning that it was OK for me to do my Esther project. Sure they're worried, but they still decided to let me do it. I'm sure G-d wants me to do this. I want to learn all I can about Esther. And find her!"

Debbie looked out the window again. The sun peeped out from behind a gigantic cloud. Its light dazzled her part of the world one more time before it sank below the horizon. A wink, she thought. "G-d," she whispered. "Help me find Esther. I just know that's one of the reasons You made me. And... help me find all the reasons."

CHAPTER SEVENTEEN

"Mmmm," Debbie said as she and Miri got out of the elevator. "Grandma Eva's apartment always smells so delicious Friday afternoon!" The scent of freshly baked bread, roasted chicken, and cake wafted through the door that Grandma Eva had left open for her girls.

When they went in, Miri headed straight for the kitchen. "It's us, Grandma Eva!" she called.

Grandma Eva hugged and kissed both girls and shepherded them into the kitchen, where she handed each of them a sliver of gooey chocolate cake on a small plate. "Just a taste," she said. "I don't want to ruin your appetites."

"Yum," Miri managed to say through a mouthful of cake. Then she went into the living room to explore one of Grandma Eva's collections. Grandma Eva had collections of books, shells and photos. She had a fish tank stocked with a variety of fish.

As soon as Miri left the kitchen, Grandma Eva took both of Debbie's hands in her own. "Debbie, I want to talk to you about your English project."

Debbie looked up at her grandmother's lined face and suddenly felt worried. She did not want to bring that old pain back to her grandmother. She did not want her to be disappointed all over again. For the first time, she really understood why her parents were so concerned. Maybe waiting and hoping made her worry too much, and it was better to give up and move on. Debbie felt a wave of sadness. She felt worried that she may cause her grandmother pain just when she wanted to help.

Grandma Eva lightly smoothed her fingers across Debbie's brow. "It's OK," she said in a reassuring voice. "Your parents just felt I should know."

Grandma Eva moved away and peeked into the oven to check the bread. "Just tell me, Debbie who are you doing this for? Because if it's for me, believe me..."

Debbie cleared her throat and hesitated before she spoke. "It's for all of us, Grandma Eva. And for Esther. Probably, though, mostly for me." Debbie paused. She had just realized what she said for the first time. "I can't get Esther out of my mind. Everything that happens in school, at home, or in Bat Mitzvah class makes me think of her and want to find her. Grandma Eva? I think what she did was the biggest sacrifice! I mean, she left her family, and she... she risked her life to save Jewish people."

"But, Grandma Eva?" Debbie said this with the deepest concern.

"Yes, dear Devorah'leh?"

"Are you upset?"

"Upset?"

"About looking for her again. I mean, maybe you don't want to start worrying again. Maybe its better not to."

"Debbie, something tells me what you are doing is something that you have to do. It seems to be part of your growing up. How can I be upset with that?"

"Grandma Eva, I..."

Debbie stopped abruptly just as Miri came in the kitchen. Debbie gave Grandma Eva a look, which Grandma Eva quickly returned. This was their business.

"Oh my goodness, look at the time!" Grandma Eva exclaimed. "It's almost sunset!"

Grandma scurried off to change for Shabbat. Miri looked down at her cream-colored velvet dress and turned around and around, happily letting the fabric twirl outward in a wide circle.

"Your dress is really nice," Debbie said with a smile.

"Yeah, I love this dress," Miri replied. "I always feel so special in it. Spe-e-cial," she sang in a made-up tune. "Special for Shabbat..."

Debbie looked down at her own outfit: a new rose-colored outfit with its grown-up straight skirt and a freshly pressed blouse. *I really did it! I saved this especially for Shabbat.* It had always seemed like a bother to rush home from school, jump in the bath, and change into nice clothes before the trips to Grandma Eva's. But now, just before Shabbat, with the delicious scent of the meal, Grandma Eva's glowing silver Shabbat candlesticks shining on the table, the clean linen tablecloth, the good china dishes... everything felt right, and she was glad she had made the effort. Just like a princess.

"You look so cool!" Miri said as Grandma Eva, wearing a blue flowered dress, bustled into the kitchen.

"Why, thank you," Grandma Eva replied, somewhat startled. "It wasn't easy finding something worthy of wearing in the presence of my two dazzling granddaughters!" She opened the oven to check the challahs one more time. They were done, and she pulled the golden loaves out of the oven. "Come now. Let's light."

They gathered in front of the candles. "Grandma," Debbie said. "Is it true that you can ask G-d for whatever you want when you light the candles?"

Miri giggled. "Like brand new roller blades?"

Grandma smiled and put her hand on Miri's head. "Well... I know this. When I light the candles, I will always have the picture of my mother in my mind as she stood before her candles, with her head covered and her hands over her eyes, whispering her own private prayer to G-d for her children. I think that moment is our own special time to feel alone with Him."

"If I don't have children, then can I pray for roller blades?" They all laughed. Debbie rolled her eyes. *Little sisters are sooo embarrassing.* Grandma hugged Miri.

First Miri lit her candle, covered her eyes, and then recited the candle-lighting prayer. "Amen!" Grandma Eva and Debbie said softly after Miri ended. Miri looked up and said, "Shabbat Shalom!"

Debbie struck a match to her candle. The wick picked up the flame with a hiss, shooting its soft glow onto the silver tray beneath the candlestick. Debbie closed her eyes. *"Baruch ata…"* She concluded the blessing and added her own silent prayer: "G-d, please bless me and Miri and Mom and Dad and Grandma Eva and all of our family and Leah and my friends and Mrs. Levy and everyone in the world with a peaceful and happy week. And, please, help me find Esther."

Grandma Eva lit her candles. Debbie watched her grandmother's face during her silent prayer, wondering what secret thoughts and wishes Grandma Eva had. As the light danced around the candlesticks, Debbie thought of that scary time so many years ago when her seasick grandmother had first unwrapped her candlesticks on the ship. *She must have felt so sad! She must have thought back to her Shabbats at home in Poland and how she lit the candles with her mother and Esther, and how they sat down to a big meal with the family all close together. She knew her life would never be the same again.*

Grandma Eva finished. Then she turned to kiss the girls and wish them a good Shabbat.

It's turned out OK for her. She's had good times and

bad times, but things turned out OK. It all must be what G-d wanted. Debbie hugged Grandma Eva.

"Who could want anything more?" Grandma Eva murmured with Debbie in her arms.

Debbie looked down at her plate, full of roasted chicken and potatoes, fruit compote, and fresh challah. Every bit was oozing with Grandma Eva's love.

"It's too much," Debbie protested as Grandma Eva added a generous piece of kugel to her plate.

Grandma Eva smiled playfully. "You should have seen Shabbat in the old country. We'd sit around the table singing for hours because we were all so stuffed we couldn't get up." She laughed. "Every time we protested to Mama that we couldn't eat another bite, she'd say that it's a mitzvah to honor the Shabbos."

Debbie looked thoughtful. "We learned at Bat Mitzvah Club that mitzvahs feed our souls the way food feeds our bodies."

"What an interesting way of putting it," Grandma Eva said. "Then tonight I feel doubly full."

She paused, then turned to Miri. Her voice grew soft. "You're probably not too young to understand this, Miri. There are times in life when G-d can seem far away." Miri's expression was serious. "When I was your age, the world felt upside down to me. But when I lit the Shabbat candles in my mother's candlesticks, I felt that G-d was close again, and it made the world turn right side up like it should be. Sometimes I'd take out the candlesticks even in the middle of the week, and they gave me hope and good feelings for the week. It's as if they carried me from Shabbat to Shabbat."

"Grandma, it's like they lit up your whole week." Debbie could hear Mrs. Levy's voice. "The whole week draws from the blessing of Shabbat, and Shabbat elevates the week." *I guess that's what Mrs. Levy must have meant.*

Grandma Eva's face shone. "Who would have known that G-d would bring me through these years until this moment right here with you? What a prize!" She squeezed Miri's hand, stood up, and began stacking the dishes.

"Now, don't let me talk on and on like this forever. Who's got room for chocolate cake?"

"No room, Grandma," Miri moaned, rubbing her stomach. "I'm so full of your good Shabbat cooking. But…" she grinned impishly, "I guess I can eat a little cake."

Grandma Eva laughed and paused at the kitchen door. "I just remembered a story my father used to tell us on Shabbat," she said. "Can the cake wait a minute, Miri?" Miri nodded gratefully. "I'll try to tell it the way he did." She put the stack of dishes down on the counter just inside the doorway, then turned and sat back down on a chair that she pulled away from the table, leaving Debbie and Miri in front of her as the audience.

"When G-d created all the animals, the bird had a complaint, and this is what she said: 'So what if I have a beautiful voice? What use is that when there is no way to escape from my enemies? All I can do is try to run away.' So G-d gave the bird two wings. But was the bird happy? No! Now she complained more bitterly than before. 'At least,' she told G-d, 'before I could run. Now these two floppy things weigh me down and I can hardly move at all!' 'Foolish creature,' G-d replied. 'With these wings you can soar away far above your enemies.' Finally the bird was happy. She started flapping her wings, she learned to look upward, and she flew away."

Grandma Eva smiled. "That's us. All we have to do is find the wings G-d gave us and use them to do our mitzvot and... we can fly!"

That night, after Miri stumbled off to bed, Debbie took down the photo album of Esther. Thumbing through the portrait of Esther's life, she felt as if she was watching Esther grow from a child into a pretty teenager with a strong look in her eye. Grandma Eva watched Debbie for a moment, then put her reading aside and crossed the room to her desk. She slid open a drawer and pulled out a fat file folder.

"Devorah," she said softly. "Maybe this will help you. Here are all the papers connected with our search for Esther. This will tell you the places we contacted. You will see as you look through these that we did find a few survivors who had information about Esther. Fellow partisans. People she saved. But everything led nowhere. I am afraid that most of these witnesses are gone now, too."

Grandma Eva shook her head.

"Thanks, Grandma," Debbie said softly, taking the file. "I'll be careful with this."

"Yes, I know," Grandma Eva said. "And if it doesn't lead anywhere, well... all you can do is your best."

CHAPTER EIGHTEEN

Their mother came to pick them up that night after the close of Shabbat. Grandma Eva walked them to the car. The first thing that Debbie noticed about her mother was the expression on her face. She had that look, the one that slid across her face just before she and Miri opened their birthday presents.

"What is it, Mom?!" Debbie exclaimed.

"Get in the car," her mother laughed. She ushered them into the car, closed the doors, and turned to kiss Grandma Eva goodbye under the bright lights at the entry to her building. "Thanks, Mother. I appreciate you keeping these two 'troublemakers' for Shabbat. I have to admit, though, it was awfully quiet around the house." She winked at Miri, who had rolled down her window and was stretching out to hug Grandma Eva one last time.

Grandma Eva smiled and hugged Miri. Debbie was wishing just a tiny bit that she was still small enough to do the same. *Anyway, I can't stand up and reach through the window like that. I don't fit.* "My pleasure," she heard Grandma say.

"Maybe you'll come to our house next week?" Debbie's mother called as she slowly drove the car out of the entry drive. Miri called out after her, "Bring your cookies!" Debbie rode home with the image of Grandma Eva smiling and waving at them in the spotlight as they drove away.

"Mom, what is it?!" Debbie pleaded as the car headed toward home.

"Come on, no fair!" Miri chimed in.

"Okay, okay, I won't keep you in suspense. I just picked up the mail before I came to get you. I brought a letter for you, Debbie."

"A letter?" complained Miri. "I thought maybe you and Daddy had decided to take us to Disney World for spring break, or something."

"If you want to read it now, I'll take the flashlight out of the glove compartment at the next red light." She was able to do it within a couple of minutes.

Debbie carefully opened the envelope. The return address was the U.S. Holocaust Museum.

I can't believe this happened so fast. It's only been a couple of weeks. The letter was dated the 29th of February, the leap day in the leap year. Her hands shook as she unfolded the letter inside. *They know something!*

Debbie leaned forward and whispered urgently to her mother. "Mom! It says they were able to trace several people who fit Esther's description." Mom was speeding up the entry ramp to the highway, and did not answer.

"Great!" Miri squealed. "That's so exciting! I can't wait to see Grandma Eva's face when she meets Esther again!" Miri stopped suddenly and let her mouth hang open. "Uh oh," she said.

"Miri! How do you know about Esther?!" Debbie asked incredulously.

"I... I just do," she answered nervously.

"You just do. You just do," Debbie said in a mocking tone. "Mom! She must have been reading my Club journal!" Miri's face went red. Debbie knew it was true.

"Miri! I'm surprised at you!"

The two sisters started pushing and shoving each other in the backseat. "Debbie! Miri!" their mother shouted.

"She started," Miri whined.

"And you don't have to finish," her mother said. "Now both of you behave. This highway is no place to stop, but I'll find a place to stop if I have to."

The two sisters moved apart and glared at each other. Debbie was really upset. "Mom? Can't I have any privacy?"

"Of course you can. And I expect your sister to honor it. It looks like Miri had a hard time resisting."

"Debbie," Miri blurted out. "I just had to find out what you were doing at the library and alone in your room so much. And..." She paused. "It's sooo exciting, isn't it?" She hugged herself. "Grandma Eva's going to be so happy. Just think, losing your only big sister!" She looked at Debbie. "Well…" she said.

Debbie could tell what her sister was thinking. She swallowed hard. *This one's for you, Mrs. Levy.* "Miri, maybe… maybe you really should have known. This is your family, too."

"Debbie, I can't believe my ears," her mother said. "You really are starting to grow up." Miri looked grateful. Debbie looked back at her letter.

"Wait a minute! They say it doesn't look like it'll be that easy. The museum doesn't have any recent information about them—just stuff from the 1950's and 1960's. They do know that one came to America after the war. One girl moved to Israel, and another's somewhere in Russia."

Debbie read further to herself.

"Come on," Miri complained. "Say it out loud!"

"Hold on, there's too much stuff," Debbie wailed. "It's hard to see. The car's too bouncy. Oh, Mom, could you read it when we get home?"

"Sure. We'll sit in the kitchen, where the light is better. We'll be home in, oh, fifteen minutes. Does that sound good?"

"Great," Debbie replied with a yawn. She was tired, but far too excited to sleep.

Mrs. Solomon finally pulled their car into the garage and turned off the engine. Miri jumped out. "I'm going to tell Daddy!" she called as she ran into the house.

"I'm telling him first!" Debbie cried out as she scrambled out of the car.

Soon after, they were all settled at the kitchen table, steaming cups of cocoa in hand. Debbie sat next to her father, who listened with little comment. Why is Dad so quiet? Maybe he doesn't like me doing this. Maybe he just let me try because he didn't want to disappoint me. Debbie's mother read the letter to herself and then summarized aloud from the beginning. "It says here that one girl never left Europe after the war because she was searching for her family. She was freed from a Nazi concentration camp after the war and spent a year in a displaced person's camp in Germany to recover her health. After that, she went in search of her family. She ended up in Russia, and the last sighting of her was in a Russian prison camp in the 1960's." She paused to sip her cocoa.

"They have an address of another inmate from the camps who resettled in Israel after being released. This person testifies that she knew someone who fit Esther's description in the Russian camp. That "Esther" often spoke of her efforts to find her family after the war, and said that she traveled around to villages now empty of their Jewish population to look for clues. She finally decided to continue her search in Israel but was denied a visa by the Soviet government. She married another refugee living in Moscow. This same witness says that this woman helped to set up a secret school for Jewish children. In the 1950's, during the worst of Stalin's anti-Jewish purges, someone informed on her and she was arrested as an enemy of the state and sent to a Siberian work camp."

"What's an enemy of the state?" asked Miri.

"It's when they don't want you going around saying things, but they won't let you go free either. So they put you in jail. Is that right, Mom?" asked Debbie.

"Basically," her mother replied. "That's what the Soviets called anyone they thought might not give the communist government their full support."

Debbie sniffled. "It's so sad. And just like our Esther, she was so strong and brave. Mom, she was so good. It's not fair that so many bad things had to happen to her."

"I don't understand it either, sweetheart," her mother replied. "Who understands how G-d runs this world—or how His creations mess it up the way we do?" She sighed.

"Mom," Debbie said. "Mrs. Levy says that there's always some good hidden in every bad, and that it's up to us to... to uncover it."

"How?"

"With our mitzvot. Grandma said lighting her Shabbat candles used to help her to do that all week. Mom? Do you think it's a mitzvah to find Esther?"

"Do I think G-d has commanded us to find her? Not exactly, but... weren't you saying the other night that it's a mitzvah to love another Jew? Aren't you doing this for Grandma?"

"Yes! So it's for sure, plain and simple."

Her father grinned at her.

Debbie pulled her knees up to her chest as she sat in the kitchen chair. She sipped from her cup, put it on the table, and said, "Keep reading, Mom."

"Debbie, don't forget, even though we feel so sorry for her, we really have no idea if the person we're reading about is our Esther. And the museum doesn't have as much information about the others. One sailed to New York in the late 1940's and is believed to have moved to California. One went to Israel. The museum gave their addresses. There are two more."

"Let's call them up," Miri said eagerly.

"It's 10 o'clock at night, Miri," Debbie said, and yawned loudly. "In some parts of the world it's the middle of the night. Besides, I have a hunch that the Esther we want is the one in the Russian prison. And maybe... maybe she didn't even survive this long." Her voice dropped.

"Debbie, we'll take this one step at a time," her father said kindly. "Don't forget how much Russia's changed in the past few years. We'll do our best to track down these Esthers. All of them." *We! He said we!* Her mother reached across the table and squeezed her oldest daughter's hand. "You'll do your best. It's your project, after all."

Debbie closed the door to her room. She put the Holocaust Museum letter on her desk and carefully placed Grandma Eva's file next to it. She took her Club journal and lay down on the bed. Suddenly the enormity of the project hit her.

"It's too hard," she wrote. "I'm only eleven. What am I doing messing around with Soviet prisons?" She yawned again, and lay her head down on her arm, the pencil still in her hand.

Debbie imagined a brave and beautiful Esther shakily aiming a pick-axe at a solid slab of rock under the harsh gaze of a prison guard. Esther, shivering as the frigid Siberian winds gusted through her ragged clothes, weakened from years of eating only bread and water, could hardly lift the axe. The guard swore and laughed at her, promising more beatings. Esther treasured something in her mind. It was a memory that survived the war, the camps, the beatings of the guards, the harsh winters. It was a picture of her family's joyous Shabbat table in the old country. She mentally kissed every member of the family. She wondered sometimes what she would do differently if she knew how the whole nightmare would turn out. But then she knew that she would still suffer, and sacrifice, and do it all over again. Because it was worth it.

Chapter Nineteen

Debbie woke up just as she had nodded off—in her clothes on top of the bed. Her Club journal and pencil had fallen to the floor. She massaged her sore neck and straightened up. It was still dark—four o'clock in the morning by the glow of the clock next to her bed. *I can't sleep. No way.* She rubbed her eyes and got up, turning on her desk lamp. The first thing she saw was the photo of Esther that Grandma Eva had given her. There was Esther, in the frame on Debbie's desk next to the lamp, with that dark hair cascading down around her lovely face. Two dark eyes peered outward at the camera and there was a trace of a smile. Something about her looked strong and hopeful. *This must be how Grandma Eva remembers her.*

Debbie cleared off the surface of her desk and spread out the papers from Grandma Eva's file. Most of what was there appeared to be copies of letters that were sent out to dozens of organizations. There were letters to other cities in America, to Germany, France and Israel, addresses in Poland and Russia—even the American Embassy in Shanghai, China! All of the letters said more or less the same thing: a description of Esther, ideas about her last known whereabouts, and a request for any information that might help reunite her with her family. Some of the copies of the letters had notations penciled in, tracking their progress. Grandma Eva or Grandpa must have written these. The letter on top of the pile said, "No news as of 20 March 1946."

Debbie shifted to the last letter, which was addressed to the Jewish Repatriation Society. The note on it said: "War Repatriation Department closed. No further tracing possible. June 7, 1965."

"Not fair!" Debbie exclaimed out loud, then she clapped her hand over her mouth. She didn't want to wake anybody up. "How could they have just stopped looking when so many people weren't found?" she whispered to herself.

"Now that's a good question." Debbie's father's voice broke into her thoughts.

"Oh, Daddy!" Debbie said, startled. "You scared me. What are you doing up?"

"Well, to be perfectly honest, I was just about to tiptoe to this very desk and borrow that file to look through it," her father answered, "Again."

"Again?"

"Sweetheart, you're not the only member of this family who's ever been on fire to find Grandma Eva's lost sister. All of us have spent more hours than we can count on the search."

"But why did you give up?"

Debbie's father looked serious. "Give up? I suppose you could call it that. We gave up. But then again, maybe you should say," he thought a moment, "we gave in."

"What's the difference?"

"I guess you can only do as much as you can. Then, when you really feel you've done all you can, you have to do a little bit more. But sometimes, you have to give in and figure that things are the way G-d wants them to be. Then we try to make peace with the situation."

"I don't think I'll ever relax as long as we don't know where Esther is," Debbie said.

Her father's face looked serious. He met her quizzical glance. "I didn't say that you won't have success. I have so much faith in you... "

"Oh, come on, Daddy. I might as well give in right now if all of you tried so hard and came up with nothing."

"I think that would be a major mistake. And anyway, I don't believe you could give up. Do the very best you can and then..."

"...do a little bit more. I heard you, Daddy." Debbie paused. "Daddy, do you think maybe the reason G-d made me was so I would find out the truth about Esther?"

"You're going to find a lot of purposes in your life, little one. And when you've really done everything you can, you'll know G-d knows you did your best. You can have peace with that, no matter what the outcome of your search is. Finding that peace with G-d inside yourself— that's the real search."

"Then, Daddy, why did you come in here tonight for Grandma Eva's file? You did your best to find Esther. You found the peace in your heart."

Debbie's father let out a quiet chuckle and then sighed, "That's the catch. We never get to just coast along, do we? It's true, I hit my limit, but now I feel I should go back and try some more. Do you want some help?"

"Daddy, I'll always take your help."

"OK. Let's take this stuff downstairs where we can spread them out on the kitchen table and we'll get those juices flowing again." He winked. "I think we could use some hot cocoa."

After an hour, they determined that most of the leads that the museum had provided matched up pretty closely with the same people that Grandma Eva had contacted years before, all with negative results.

"That leaves only three," said Debbie.

"Only three!? Hey," Debbie's father exclaimed, "don't look so unhappy. Look how far you've come. In just a few weeks, you've come up with more than anyone has in years. A lot has happened in the last ten years. The Iron Curtain came down. This new museum was built. And a lot of this new information is now on computers. Maybe you can do some of your search on the Internet. All we could do is send out dozens and dozens of letters, sometimes to people and places that no longer existed. The fact that you've turned up three new leads in such a short time gives me new hope, Debbie. Let's write to them all! Tonight." He consulted his watch. "I think we can get out three letters before the sun comes up."

CHAPTER TWENTY

"My life is falling apart!" Debbie moaned to herself. She flopped down on her bed and rolled herself up into a ball. "How could I be so stupid?" she whispered.

Why didn't I know better? Every time someone at school breaks up with a best friend, I always look at them and say, "No way! Not me! I'd never act so mean. If my friend were mad at me, I'd figure out a way to forgive them." Some plan.

But how do you act mature when your friend won't? I'm hurting my very best friend in the whole entire world. And now she considers me her number one enemy!

"I hate you, Debbie Solomon!" Leah screamed. "Never call me again. Never!" she added as she slammed down the phone.

That was a whole week ago, and it was the last time they spoke.

Debbie was hurt. She missed Leah so much. She felt like she had not smiled in a year. She felt like her heart was breaking.

And the absolutely stupidest thing is it's all my fault.

She knew better, but she couldn't resist. When Rachel Levine offered to take her along to the ice show with their family, Debbie said "yes" even though the ice show was on the same Sunday afternoon that she and Leah had made plans for a shopping trip to a downtown mall. Leah's mother was going to take them and let them wander through all the stores and look for shoes to match The Dress.

But then along came that ice show ticket like candy on a stick, dangling teasingly in front of her eyes. It was a once-in-a-lifetime opportunity. It only took a moment for Debbie to swallow hard and reply, "Wow, great, Rachel! I'd love to go. What time should I be ready?" Shopping could wait. She could go anytime to the mall with Leah.

Practically as soon as Debbie hung up with Rachel, the phone rang again. It was Leah and she wanted to discuss their outing. Debbie changed the subject as much as she could but Leah kept pressing Debbie until she couldn't avoid it anymore.

Debbie felt grateful they were talking on the phone. Face to face, she would never have been able to hide her expression. She knew without looking that her face was red from embarrassment.

Debbie paused. To her own ears it sounded as if she was

babbling. "Uh… sorry, Leah. I can't go with you. I have to…uhh… I have to help my grandmother with, um, spring-cleaning. I promised." A big, fat lie. She felt horrible and ashamed. *I hope it worked.* Then she remembered. *Uh oh. Leah's going to come up with one of her plans.*

"Oh, come on, Debbie. Tell your grandmother you'll help her out one day after school. What's the difference when you go over there?"

"She's really counting on me, Leah. I…" Debbie couldn't come up with a good answer. "I can't let her down."

Debbie wasn't prepared for what came next: "I'll come along!" Leah offered. "With the two of us working, we'll get everything done in the morning. I'll get my mother to drive us to your grandmother's. It's not very far from your grandmother's apartment to the mall. See, I've got everything figured out!"

Debbie felt panicked. "Uh, uh no, Leah. I don't think so," she stammered.

"Why not?" Leah sounded hurt.

"Well," Debbie thought fast, "Well, my grandmother said she wanted to spend some time alone with me, since it's almost my Bat Mitzvah and everything."

Silence on Leah's end. Debbie knew that her explanation wasn't convincing.

"Yeah, okay, Debbie," Leah said in a low voice. Then came Leah's bombshell. "It's Rachel, isn't it? You made plans with her. Instead of me. Even though you and I had these plans for weeks." Leah's voice gained strength.

"Admit it, Debbie."

Debbie couldn't answer. The palms of her hands were wet with perspiration. Her heart pounded. She knew she had to tell the truth. "Leah, I'm sorry," Debbie whispered.

But her apology didn't help.

Debbie couldn't remember any other time in her life that passed so slowly.

She felt terrible through the entire ice show. The skaters were beautiful, and she gasped along with everyone else when her favorite skater successfully landed a triple toe loop, but she felt like a criminal the entire day. She felt as if she had stolen something big—a fantastic friendship—and broken it into little tiny pieces. *It wasn't worth an ice show. It wasn't even worth the Olympics!*

After the ice show, when Rachel's mother invited Debbie to go with them for pizza, Debbie replied that her parents expected her to come right home. Another lie. She said it because she could not bear pretending any longer that she was having fun. But even the strain of pretending that she was having a good time was better than the loneliness that hit her as soon as she waved good-bye and closed her front door behind her.

No one was home. Debbie felt so alone. She tried to read for a while, but she couldn't concentrate. She paced around the house. "So, big deal that I went someplace with Rachel," she told herself out loud. "How could Leah be such a baby?" *Leah's so immature! Who wants to hang* around with someone so small, anyway?

I do. I want to hang around with her. More than any-thing. Debbie wanted to cry. Then it hit her. She remembered something Mrs. Levy said at the Bat Mitzvah Club: The mind rules over the heart. *My heart won this time. Now it's time for my Jewish soul to take charge. OK. I'll stop feeling sorry for myself and decide to do something.* Debbie walked in determined strides to the telephone, picked it up, and dialed.

"Oh, hello, Debbie," Leah's mother answered. "Leah's out today with a group of her friends. I think they went to the downtown mall."

"Th… thank you, Mrs. Fisher." Her heart sank. She quickly hung up. *So it's true. Leah doesn't need me or miss me at all.*

Debbie threw herself into the big old arm chair in the den. Her thinking chair. *Rachel's neat to hang around with and she makes me think about different things. She talks about things I never talk with Leah about! Like how to have a normal life when you're so busy competing in sports—and how she manages to have a normal life. But there's one problem: Rachel isn't Leah. Leah's like… like my other half. I can't spend even a week without her jokes and her crazy ideas!*

Every day after that, Debbie left notes at Leah's locker at school. She wrote "I'm so sorry. I miss you," and she signed her name and drew a smiling face. Another time she wrote, "My heart tricked me so I didn't think, but next time I'll think. I promise!"

But there was no response. Leah snubbed Debbie in the classes that they had together, and when Debbie sat at their usual lunch table, Leah got up and moved. The other girls at the table felt awkward and didn't know what to say to Debbie or Leah, and when Debbie tried to join in conversation they all fell silent. It made Debbie feel terrible. She felt that all of her friends had sided with Leah, and she didn't blame them at all.

Every night, Debbie called Leah's house, and every night Leah's mother or father answered and apologetically told Debbie that Leah wouldn't come to the phone. "She can't come?" Debbie asked sadly. "It's not that, Debbie," Mrs. Fisher answered. "She can, but she won't. I'm really sorry." *I won't give up on her. I won't give up on our friendship.* But Leah's determination was wearing her down.

CHAPTER TWENTY-ONE

If only something in my life would work out. Every day, I race home from school to see the mail, but all I find is bills or letters for my parents or junk mail. One of her "Esther letters" came back stamped "Return to Sender: Addressee Unknown."

What could be taking Esther so long to answer? Maybe the letter got lost or she moved and the post office doesn't know her new address. Or maybe my letter was such a shock that she doesn't know what to do next.

There was one possibility that Debbie pushed out of her mind. She refused to imagine the possibility that Esther could not be found. Every time that thought popped into Debbie's head, she pushed it out again. *I won't think about it. I'll just keep trying my hardest, like I promised Dad.*

Debbie left the day's disappointing batch of mail on the

189

hall table and went up to her room. She lay down on her bed and stared at the pebbly white ceiling of her room. She had slept poorly the previous night, tossing and turning, thinking of Leah. Now she pushed the image of her friend out of her mind. Dreamily, she imagined herself greeting Esther. How she wished that could happen!

Suddenly, Debbie heard a doorbell ring. She ran to the door, somehow anticipating exciting news. It was a special delivery letter! With shaking hands she tore open the outer cover before she remembered to look at the return address. She could not believe her eyes. She swiftly took out the letter and deciphered the old-fashioned handwriting.

"Dear Debbie,

I received your letter with great joy. Thank G-d you did not give up in your search! Your courage to continue will reunite our family..."

"Debbie. Wake up. It's dinnertime. Don't you want to come in?"

Debbie was still sprawled across her bed. She turned over and looked up, bewildered. "Who? Oh, I must have fallen asleep. Oh, Mommy, I had such a good dream."

"What was it?"

"Mommy, Esther sent me a letter. And she promised that our family will be together again. She said, oh let me think, she said 'Your courage to continue will reunite our family.' I wish it were true!"

Her mother sat down on the bed next to her. "Just a minute. Maybe this is a good message. I think you must have had some real courage to continue your search. You had to face your teacher and your parents, and you had to figure out how to do something that was completely new to you. And you didn't give in. Maybe the Esther in your dream was right." She smiled mysteriously, and then slowly pulled two envelopes out of her pocket. "Which reminds me of something that came in today's mail."

"Yeah, those magazine sweepstakes. I saw those, too," Debbie said. "I always send them back but I never win." Her mother gently pressed the envelopes into her hand.

Debbie scanned the postmarks. One letter was from Israel and the other read Brooklyn, New York. All of a sudden, Debbie felt short of breath. "Wha-what?" Debbie said wonderingly. "The Esthers! And two in one day!"

"I've been holding onto them all day waiting to give them to you. I wanted to be here with you when you opened them. Isn't this exciting?"

"Oh, Mom, I'm nervous. I can't believe it!" Debbie cried. "Can we call Dad?"

"I called your father right away. He walked out of an important meeting at work twice to call and see what's in the letters. We'll call him as soon as you open them."

Debbie's hand shook as she carefully tore open the Israeli envelope first. She read the letter. "This one says: Hello to you in America! I received your most interesting letter about your relative. I know how hard it is to lose someone in the war. I am the only one in a family of eight brothers and sisters who survived.

"This handwriting is hard to read." Debbie read on to herself, squinting at the words.

"She says she met several people in Europe after the war that might fit Esther's description, but she says there must be some mistake because her name is Miriam. She says 'Good luck in your search.' And she wants to know if we know her cousins, the Charnes, who settled in our area after the war."

"Charnes?" Debbie asked. "Who are the Charnes?"

"Well, maybe she means that nice elderly woman who reads stories to the children at the synagogue on Shabbat. Her name is Mrs. Charnes."

"Wow, Mrs. Charnes was in the Holocaust? I never knew. I wonder who else we know who was there?" Debbie mused as she folded up the letter and put it back into its envelope.

"Maybe we'll have better luck with this one," her mother said as she held up the Brooklyn envelope. "You read it, Mommy," Debbie said.

Debbie watched her mother's expression as it went from a frown to a smile. "What is it?" she asked in a voice filled with excitement.

"Well!" her mother stated. "This woman says she was born in Russia in 1953 and her mother was named Esther. She said that the description we sent to her sounds familiar but she's not entirely sure."

"Not sure about her own mother? Why in the world not?" asked Debbie.

"Well," her mother continued, "Her name is Lena. She says she is the daughter of a woman who was sent to Siberia. She says that she was very young when it happened and she never saw her mother again. She says that her father was so sad about her mother's imprisonment that he could never speak much about her. 'My father passed away many years ago,'" she read aloud. "'But he never stopped telling me how brave my mother was. She never gave up on G-d even with all her hard times. And she never gave up her hope of finding her family again.'"

"Go on, go on," Debbie implored. "Don't stop there."

"Lena says that in Russia it was impossible to get information from other places in the world. After her mother was arrested, the KGB, the Russian secret police, closely watched her family. She says that after that, they stopped trying to find relatives in the free world. After the communist government fell in Russia, they had an opportunity to come to America.

"'I now live in Brooklyn with my husband and children. My husband has two sisters and a brother who also live here with their families. My life is filled with family, but I never felt complete without my mother and her family. I never felt complete because I did not know the fates of my grandparents and aunts and uncles.' She ends by saying that she's eager to hear from us and discover if we are long-lost relatives."

Debbie sat in stunned amazement. Her mother ducked out to answer the hallway telephone. After a brief conversation, she quickly came back to Debbie's room. "That was your father again. I told him about the letter. He thinks we should wait to call Grandma Eva until after we investigate this woman a little." Her mother paused. "Now don't get that look on your face. You won't die if you don't speak to her right this very moment. We'll talk it all over with her when she comes over for Shabbat."

Debbie's mother left her room. Debbie ran for the telephone. *I've got to tell Leah the news!* She dialed all the numbers but the last one. Then she remembered. *Look what I've done! I can't call Leah. She'll just hang up on me.* Sorrowfully, Debbie put the receiver back on the hook.

Debbie's family had never eaten dinner as quickly as they did that night. It seemed like Debbie's mother had no sooner placed the platter of tuna casserole on the table than everyone's plate was cleaned of any trace of dinner. Even Miri was quiet as the girls waited to hear what their parents thought about the letters.

"The letter seems genuine," mused Debbie's father. "You know, you never can tell what people are after when they claim to be your long-lost relatives. But considering that this woman is responding to Debbie's letter, it's certainly safe to contact her by phone."

"I just thought of something, Daddy. If she really is related, how come she never searched for us?"

"Don't forget how long it's taken us to find her. She was

living in Russia until recently. And apparently her father told her very little. She didn't know any details that would help her find us, like names or dates or hometowns. I think we should call."

The whole family gathered around the living room phone as Debbie's father called the number that Lena wrote in her letter. "Ringing, ringing," Debbie's father said aloud, counting with his fingers. "Hello, may I speak to Lena, please?"

Debbie swallowed a squeal of excitement and leaned up close to her father in hopes of overhearing the conversation. Her father put on the speaker phone.

"Yes, hello, this is Jacob Solomon. Yes, Jacob Solomon. You don't know me, but I believe you received a letter from my daughter, Debbie. Yes, your reply came this afternoon. Yes, yes I will. Oh, I see!" He whispered to Debbie, "She's on the phone, but I have to switch off the speaker. Too much echo!"

They could only watch their father as he listened for several minutes, his face composed and serious. He asked many questions, and Debbie felt she almost couldn't stand waiting to hear the answers. Several times he smiled, but there was a certain formality in his voice, as if he was being cautious. Finally, he hung up the receiver. Then he was silent. He looked over at the others, staring at him, waiting.

"Well?" they finally asked simultaneously.

"Well, indeed," he replied. "Now we can't yet know anything one-hundred percent for sure, but..."

"But what, Daddy?" broke in Debbie and Miri in unison.

"It's possible Debbie has found the key to the mystery of Esther."

CHAPTER TWENTY-TWO

"And if it's so, my most amazing daughter," Mr. Solomon continued as he lifted Debbie's chin with his finger, "You have accomplished something our family has tried and failed for thirty years. We'll all remember this for the rest of our lives." Debbie felt a thrill to her toes. Could it be? Oh, could it be?

Debbie's father recounted his conversation with Lena. "Basically," he said, "she repeated the information that she wrote to Debbie. There's a lot that she doesn't know about our Esther since she was so young when Esther disappeared. But the pieces that she does know fit what we are looking for. Somehow, I believe her. It's hard not to believe that her mother is our Esther. She thinks so."

"Did Lena know anything about where Esther is now?" asked Debbie.

"It's been so long since she's had any information about her mother," he said. "Since she moved to America, she said that she hasn't tried at all. Lena's father was her only family, and he passed away years ago. She says that the last time she inquired about her mother was more than five years ago. The Russian government told her that they had no records at all of Esther. Lena thinks that they didn't really take the time to check. She says that her efforts to get information were thwarted by the missing persons agency there. Lena says that so many people were sent to Siberia or secretly killed in all the years of communist rule. Then the borders started opening up after the government fell. A lot of people want the same type of information that she wants. The new government just can't keep up with all the requests."

"So is there a chance that we can find out something now?" Debbie asked.

"Well," her father replied, "Lena said she was actually planning to send more requests for information. Then she received Debbie's letter and she mailed off those new requests the same day. But she said that it could take weeks or even months to hear anything from the new Russian government, and perhaps the message will be that it has no information at all."

It was Friday night. The household was calm after the frenzied week of work and school and the interesting letters and telephone calls. The family relaxed around the dining table. Now was the time. They had decided not to tell Grandma the news until this Shabbat dinner. Mr. Solomon wanted Debbie to tell her grandmother face to face and not over the telephone.

A tear glistened in the corner of Grandma Eva's eye when Debbie told her about Lena. Debbie noticed that tear and it upset her a little, but Debbie continued telling the story about Lena, and by the end, Grandma Eva was smiling.

"It's Shabbat—the one night I can't pick up the phone and call this Lena myself," Grandma Eva said. "She could very well be my niece. I think if I speak to her, I'll know for sure if her mother is our Esther. Even though Lena was a little girl when her mother left, she'll have to remember some things, things only I know about Esther. Esther's funny nicknames for everything around her. The color of her eyes. Things like that."

Maybe Lena will look like her mother. Then Grandma Eva will know for sure. "Grandma Eva, I'm sorry I didn't tell you right when I found out. Mommy and Daddy said..."

"They were right, Debbie. And of course, you must listen to your parents," Grandma Eva replied. "I hope that you've actually found my niece, and maybe even Esther. If I could call right away, maybe I would find out this isn't Esther's daughter." She sipped her tea. "Yes, they are right in waiting. It is best that I go to sleep with this wonderful news in my head." She paused a few moments. "And if I am disappointed, at least I had a lovely Shabbos full of hope." She smiled and hugged her granddaughter close.

It was only since the girls moved to Jewish schools that Grandma Eva had begun spending an occasional Shabbat in their home. That was when they began to keep kosher. At first, Debbie thought that the Shabbat day would drag on forever. But it didn't, because Grandma Eva was with them. After coming home from synagogue, the family gathered for a late Shabbat lunch on Saturday afternoon. Grandma Eva told stories that she had heard at her parents' Shabbat table. Debbie and Miri were so caught up in the stories that they didn't realize that the sun had set on the short, winter day. Shabbat was over.

Grandma Eva went to the window and peered around a window shade at the darkness outside. "Goodness! Looks like it's time for Havdalah," she said. "And then that phone call."

"I almost forgot!" Debbie said. *Sometimes I don't want Shabbat with Grandma Eva to be over.*

"Shavuah Tov!" her father called out. "Come into the dining room for Havdalah."

Debbie and Miri held up the braided candle together. Their father carefully recited the blessing that divided Shabbat from the week ahead. He recited the blessing over the wine and another over the spices, and then he passed around the spice box for everyone to sniff. Debbie could almost hear Mrs. Levy talking about Havdalah. "The sweet scent of cloves gives us a week full of sweetness." The family looked to the burning candle. "For bringing brightness into the world." Debbie carefully dipped the candle into the wine. With a hiss the light went out and for a moment, they stood in the dark. "Shavuah Tov!" they said to one another. *Oh, let it be a good week. Let it be one.*

Miri switched on the lights. "Are you going to call Lena now, Grandma Eva?" she asked.

"First let's all pitch in and help your mother clean up the dishes," Grandma Eva replied. "Then I'll call."

"You mean we have to wait even longer?" cried Debbie and Miri almost in unison.

"Maybe you girls will work more quickly this way," Grandma Eva said with a smile.

"Thanks, Mom," Mrs. Solomon said. "Great strategy."

The girls raced around the kitchen washing and drying the mound of dishes. When everything was cleaned up and put away, Debbie and Miri surrounded Grandma Eva. "It's time!" Miri shouted, dancing around her grandmother.

Everyone hovered near Grandma Eva as she picked up the phone. She slowly looked over her eager audience. "I hate to disappoint all of you," she said, cupping her hand over the receiver. "But I'm going to need some privacy. May I use the bedroom phone?"

Debbie and Miri groaned. Mr. and Mrs. Solomon quickly nodded. Grandma Eva caressed Debbie's cheek. "I'll be right back," she whispered to her.

The family sat in tense silence. Ten minutes later Grandma Eva reappeared in the bedroom doorway.

"Well???" everyone asked.

Her cheeks were flushed, and her eyes were bright.

"Very nice woman," she began.

"Well???" came another chorus.

"...for a niece," she finished. For a moment, they all looked at her in stunned silence, and then they whooped with joy. "Yes!!!" "Yes!!!!" Debbie and Miri cried. They grabbed each other. They jumped and danced. Mr. Solomon whirled Miri around in a circle. Mrs. Solomon simply hugged her mother close for a long, long time. Debbie could not remember such joy. Grandma Eva quietly beamed at them all. "I think you've actually done it, my little Debbie. You've solved the mystery at last." Grandma Eva folded her granddaughter in her arms and hugged her tightly. "What a wonderful gift you've given me. I can't believe it," she said again and again.

"Me neither," Debbie replied.

"Here's the story," said Grandma Eva, waiting for everyone to quiet down. *She's patient, like Mrs. Levy.* "I heard Lena's tale. Poor girl, she's had such a hard time. And to think that we could have been helping her these last few years and we didn't even know she existed! But I'm convinced: I asked her a few questions, and she remembered certain things about her mother that only a daughter could know."

"Like what?" Mrs. Solomon asked.

"There was a lullaby my mother used to sing to us when we were babies. You'll remember it, dear. I sang it to you when you were a baby. Lena was able to hum it to me. She also knew details she didn't know she knew. When Esther used to tuck her into bed, she told Lena the same stories that I told you over and over about my childhood. Also, Lena remembered a few family nicknames and things like that." She paused and said thoughtfully, "I invited Lena to come here with her family."

"You did!" Miri shrieked. "When?"

"As soon as possible. Anyway, this all might not work out so soon. People do have to work. But Lena's going to talk with her husband and call us back tonight. It's possible they can't come soon because of his job."

This is absolutely the best. This is even better than my swimming victory. And the best part is seeing Grandma happy. I feel so good because I did it. I didn't give up. And now, after so much and so long, we found our family. But the happiness still wasn't complete.

"Grandma Eva," she asked hesitantly. "What about Esther?"

"Oh, Debbie, Lena is Esther!"

Debbie gasped. "What? You mean Esther's alive?"

"No, no," Grandma Eva quickly replied. "That we don't know. What I mean is, if this Lena really is Esther's daughter, Lena is Esther like you are your mother. Lena is as close as I can get to Esther without having the real thing."

"Honey," she said gently, touching Debbie's face, "this is difficult for me to actually say, but Esther can't possibly have survived that Siberian work camp. But we do have more details about her now, and we can launch an all-out investigation," she paused, "and then finally let her rest in peace."

"But what if that government never replies again? How can we ever be sure Esther's gone? How can we even think of giving up on her?" Debbie began to cry. "Esther could still be there, digging the frozen ground all day and eating crusts of bread and water." Now she was really crying. The tears streaked her face and she was shaking with her sobs. She pictured her miserable great-aunt, desperate for her family to find her, barely holding on to her life.

Grandma Eva grabbed Debbie and squeezed her tight to her chest. "Child, child!! We won't forget her," Grandma Eva said quietly. "We won't forget." Debbie returned Grandma Eva's embrace. After a long time in her grandmother's comforting arms, her sobbing stopped. Then she got up and went to bed. For a long time she lay motionless on her bed, eyes closed, awake but dreaming.

CHAPTER TWENTY-THREE

"I'm no good with kids," Leah complained as Debbie dragged her toward the entrance of the Children's Home. "I don't even baby-sit. What do I do with them? Ask their opinions whether I should cut my hair with layers or bangs? C'mon, Deb, let's skip this meeting. We'll tell Mrs. Levy that your mother was sick and I had to help you make dinner and watch Miri!"

"Forget it, Leah," Debbie answered with a huge smile. "None of your crazy plans this time!"

Debbie was thrilled to be back together with Leah. She wasn't sure what had finally done it, she just knew that she had succeeded in wearing Leah down. She showered Leah with notes and apologies, and even baked her a batch of chocolate-chip cookies.

Finally, one morning, after two-and-a-half excruciating

weeks of being ignored, Leah showed up at their usual morning meeting place and joined Debbie in the walk to school with no comment about the fight. In fact, when Debbie tried to bring it up and apologize all over again, Leah stopped her.

"Enough," Leah said, raising her arm with a hand up, as if to stop a truck from running her down. "Let's just forget it." It made Debbie wonder, though. Did that mean they should just forget Rachel? Was Leah saying that she was willing to pretend Rachel didn't exist? *That's not what I want! I want her to accept Rachel, and not just "forget it."*

Debbie's heart was pounding. "Leah, I..."

"Yeah?"

"I... I invited Rachel to join the Bat Mitzvah Club. She didn't even have a party or anything!"

Leah stopped still. She put her arms on her hips and glared at Debbie. Debbie felt really nervous. She did not know what to think. *Oh no. She's really going to get angry now. Better get this over with.*

She took a deep breath. "So—she's coming today. She's probably already here."

Suddenly, Leah's glare turned into a mischievous smile. "Cool!" she said, and the two burst out laughing. Together they continued to school.

The girls walked into the Children's Home and joined the other Bat Mitzvah Club members milling around in the lobby. Very soon Mrs. Levy swept through the doors, two toddlers in tow. "Sorry I'm late everyone!" she called out.

Mrs. Levy bent down to take off their hoods and unzip their jackets. Then she straightened up to the sight of several surprised faces. "Yes, they're mine," she laughed. "My babysitter couldn't make it today so the twins had to come along."

Twins! I never even thought of her having a husband, and she has twins!

"Rebecca and Benjamin," she said to her children, "meet the famous Bat Mitzvah Club you've heard so much about." The twins, dressed in matching turtlenecks and denim overalls, smiled obligingly.

"Look at those little teeth," Leah marveled. "They're so cute!"

The club members descended on the twins. Rachel stood quietly on the side, not yet familiar enough with everyone to join them in fawning over the tots. Benjamin laughed at the attention but Rebecca let out a sudden shriek and buried her face in her mother's legs.

"I think there are some other children waiting for us," Mrs. Levy said.

The meeting room was up a flight of stairs. The girls clattered up together and entered a large room. The room was empty except for a large mat strewn with toys and three rows of chairs set up across from a speaker's table where a young woman stood. She gestured for them to sit.

"This is Mrs. Blasser, the assistant director of the Children's Home," Mrs. Levy said. "Before you meet the children, she will tell you about the facility."

Mrs. Blasser was trim and agile looking, apparently accustomed to work, wearing blue jeans and tennis shoes. Debbie pictured her on one knee with a child. But Mrs. Blasser's voice was business-like. *I'll bet they all behave around her.*

"The children who live here range in age from three to nine. While there are many, many families who want to adopt babies, the sad truth is that older children are much harder to place. Some of the children who are here lost their parents fairly recently."

"And many of our children have parents, but they were placed here after it was decided by judges and courts that their parents weren't able to take care of them and there was nobody else. There are many reasons for this, such as sickness, poverty or abuse. And, we do have a few children who themselves were so difficult that their own parents placed them here. Usually children whose parents can't manage to raise them are either mentally or physically handicapped, in which case they need a different type of facility, but it's not always the case. If we feel we can reach the child, we will accept them."

Mrs. Blasser paused. "Regardless of the reason why our children ended up here, we are dedicated to providing them with a healthy, safe, and loving home. Our social workers, doctors, and teachers work with all the children to help them heal their past and learn how to face their futures as happy and normal children."

"Our hope is that you will be inspired by your visit here.

You will see how you can make a difference in a child's life." She paused and looked around.

"You are all young women. We want you to understand now how important you will be to your family when you become a mother. We want you to see for yourselves the difference your time and attention will make for your child's life."

"Of course, I also wouldn't mind if some of you decided to spend time volunteering here as big sisters. We always need volunteers to spend time with our children."

Debbie tried to imagine life without parents. Then she looked at Rachel sitting on the front row. Once again she tried to imagine having a mother who loved her, but who was too overwhelmed with her life to really show it. She couldn't do it. When she tried, she felt as if there was a hollow place in her chest.

Mrs. Levy stood up, flanked by little Rebecca and Benjamin. "Thank you, Mrs. Blasser," she said.

She reached down to pat her babies' heads as they began to toddle off toward the toy area in the corner of the room. "Yesterday I came here to see the place and plan our session here. Looking at the children in their play area made me think. I want to ask: When you are grown and have children, will they be your only interest? Will you be involved in anything else?"

There was silence. Debbie was shy to answer in this place, without the privacy of their regular meeting room, and with Mrs. Blasser listening in. She supposed the others felt the same way. But she saw some heads shaking "no."

"Yocheved?"

"I want to be a doctor."

"And what about your children? Will you love them? Will you have time for that?"

"Of course I will!" Yocheved sputtered. Debbie was listening keenly. *This doesn't sound like the real Mrs. Levy.*

One by one, Mrs. Levy brought out the girls' voices. Sarah wanted to be a lawyer. Ruthi asserted, "I want to be a mother. Period. Just like my Mom is for me." Allison, in her strong manner, challenged Mrs. Levy.

"What does one thing have to do with the other? I can learn a profession and do things and still have kids!" She sounded angry. "I would never neglect my kids!"

"Wait a minute. Wait a minute." Mrs. Levy smiled mysteriously. "I just want to ask one question. Are other things in life besides children—friends, careers, hobbies— meaningful to you? You all sound like you are telling me they are." The girls nodded, and murmured "yes."

"What do they do for you?"

Silence.

"What do they do for you now in your life?"

Silence.

"Do you have friends and hobbies?" There was laughter. "Of course!" many answered.

"Debbie, do you have a hobby?"

"Sort of. I mean, I think of swimming as more than a hobby, but..."

"Do you have friends?"

"Yes." She smiled.

"Why?"

"Why?"

"Yes, why? I mean, what do you gain from your hobby? And what do you gain from having friends?"

Debbie tried to think of what she would write in her journal if she had her journal there. She slowly started to compose her words.

"When I swim, I keep finding out things I never knew I could do before. And from my friends I get... well, I'm not lonely. And I just like them."

"So you learn about yourself, and your life becomes more pleasant?"

"Yes."

"But what if... what if you spent so much time with your friends that you forgot to go to school?" Everyone laughed again. *What if my friend convinces me not to go to school?*

"I'd get in trouble. And my grades would go way down."

"And what if you spent so much time swimming that you didn't do your homework? Would it be the same? Would you get in trouble and would your grades go down?"

"Yes."

"So you've got friends and hobbies, and you really like them. AND you go to school. Which is the main thing?"

"Well, I guess I have to pay attention to school first. If I go to a friend's house before I do my homework, that can make trouble for me."

"OK, so let's pretend you're grown up now. You still have friends and hobbies. But now, instead of school, you have two beautiful children. Can you put your friends and hobbies first? Isn't it OK, now?" The room was buzzing. Everyone had something to say.

Melissa got the first word in. "No! I mean, what if they were hungry? Who would take care of her children?"

"Oh... she could get a babysitter."

"It's not the same!" Allison wailed, always the bold one.

"So... maybe she shouldn't have friends and hobbies? Maybe she shouldn't have a job, especially one that she loves? Maybe she'd love those things more than her children!"

"Yes! I mean, no! I mean... oh, I don't know. Let me think."

"Amy?" Mrs. Levy nodded at Amy, who had been waiting patiently with her hand up.

"Mrs. Levy? I don't see what the big deal is. I mean, if I can have friends and hobbies now and not neglect my schoolwork, I can do other things and have kids—and not neglect them. I mean, they'd be my priority."

"Priority? What a great word, Amy! It's been singing in my head and I've been waiting for someone to say it! Are children a priority?"

"Yes!" Everyone agreed.

"Priority means what comes first. Our children must come first! Is that what you are telling me?"

Amy nodded.

"So tell me, Amy. Can't someone love and care for their children, even if their children are not their priority? What if that were so? What if a person really loves their friends, their hobbies and their job more than their children, but still always makes sure that their children have food and clothing and everything they need? How does that make you feel when I say that?"

Silence.

"Imagine yourself one of those children. Close your eyes and think about it. How do you feel?"

"I'm not happy."

"Why?"

"I feel sort of... lonely."

"What do you need from your mother that you're not getting? Remember—we're pretending Amy's a child whose parents like many other things better than they like her."

"I need—attention."

"What does that mean? What do you want?"

"Attention. I want them interested in my school work."

"Anyone else? What if you were Amy?"

Many hands went up.

"I want them to listen to me."

"Yes."

"And teach me things."

"Yes?"

"And play games with me! And take me places."

"Yes!"

One hand was raised. It was Rachel.

"Yes?" Mrs. Levy said. "What's your name? You're new, aren't you?"

Debbie looked sideways at Leah. "Mrs. Levy, this is Rachel Levine," she said. Leah had a funny, plastered smile on her face, as if she was trying hard to be extra friendly. It made her look strange. *At least she's trying to be nice.*

Rachel waited patiently. "Mrs. Levy, it's just not always like that."

"Not always like what?"

"Well, some parents want to give their children attention, but it's not their choice. Sometimes their life is too hard, and when they get home, they're too tired, or hassled, or something."

It seemed as if Rachel had opened a door and a flood came through. A lot of girls were talking at once. Mrs. Levy waited for the talk to sort itself out.

"My mother works on her feet all day, and when she comes home, she doesn't want to get up for anything!"

"If someone really loves their child, they'll pay attention to them no matter what!"

"Some kids are too obnoxious to look at. You should see my little brother."

"When my father was in the middle of the tax season, he didn't talk to us for a week."

"I'm gonna be waiting for my kids when they get home every day."

The comments went on in a jumble. Mrs. Levy waited

until they quieted. The girls knew now what she wanted when she got that patient look on her face.

"Rachel, can parents choose whether or not to pay attention to their children?"

"Well... that's what I meant. Sometimes yes, and sometimes no. Even if they really would like to. Like, they can be too tired or worried or something to make themselves do it. And, well, it sounded like you were saying everyone should just plan to make their kids their priority and the kids will automatically get enough attention, but that's just not always true."

Debbie noticed that Leah was watching Rachel with real interest. *Rachel thinks old. She can say things nobody else here would think of.* She loved the way that she and Leah often noticed the same things. *She's going to like Rachel for the same reasons I do. She just needs to give it a chance.*

"Mrs. Blasser?"

Mrs. Blasser looked up, surprised.

"Mrs. Blasser, do you ever get any children here like that?"

"Like what?"

"Children whose parents really, really feel that their children are their top priority, but they are too busy and tired to take care of them very well."

"Well, it can happen, if the parents' problems are really overwhelming, but almost never. A child in that situation usually grows up quickly and helps the parents a lot. A child who is truly loved usually feels their parents' love in spite of everything and comes out OK in the end."

As Mrs. Blasser spoke, Mrs. Levy was watching Rachel. Her look was long and her brow was somewhat creased. *Mrs. Levy looks like she understands about Rachel's family. I wonder if she knows them?*

"For Jewish parents, having a child means being partners with G-d. When G-d wanted to give the Torah to the Jews, He would only accept the children as the guarantors, because they are the most precious. The children are the future for the Jewish people and for the Torah.

"Some of the children in this Home did not get any attention. Their parents did not love them as much as they loved other things. Some of the children were treated very badly. They are deeply hurt. What if it were you?"

The girls stared at her. They seemed shocked. Mrs. Levy continued. "My greatest wish for every one of you is that you fulfill your dreams, have beautiful children, and always hold them as your brightest treasure. Being a good parent will be your best and hardest accomplishment, beyond anything else you do."

An hour later, Debbie and Leah were exhausted.

"I thought I was in good shape," Leah panted to Debbie as she tumbled a laughing three-year-old over on a mat. The child wore baggy pants that were slipping down as he tumbled. Leah stood him up and gently tugged his pants back up. "Hold still just a second,

Robbie," she said. "You don't want to lose these, do you?" Robbie stood still obediently, but briefly. There were red spots on his round cheeks.

"I thought I was in good shape, too," Debbie said. Debbie was taking a break. She stood over the mat, watching the action. Not far from Leah was Rachel, who had settled down with a picture book and three small children. One of them was in her lap. Rachel's arm was on the shoulder of the child sitting to her left.

"You know," Leah said, waving at Rachel to get her to look up from the book. "You're pretty good with them."

Rachel smiled at her and went back to the book. She seemed to be getting the children to "read" to her.

Debbie's jaw dropped open. "Leah, you?"

Leah raised her chin in mock defiance, grinning. "Don't be jealous, Debbie," she said. "You know, I can have more than one friend at a time." Then they both burst out laughing.

"Well, OK," Debbie said through her giggles. "Maybe I can share. I'll see." Rachel looked at both of them as if she did not have a clue what was going on. Debbie could not begin to explain. Leah turned back to Robbie.

"Robbie, look! Let's join them and see the picture book!" Leah led him over to sit with Rachel and her group.

Debbie looked around at the roomful of children. *Now that they're playing, they look like any kids in the world.* But it had taken enormous effort to get the games started. One boy scribbled dark, foreboding marks on sheets of paper. He sat in a corner with a black crayon, his long bangs hanging in his eyes, and rocked back and forth as he scribbled. And he looked too old to be scribbling.

She tried to chat with one little girl, but the child stared down at her shoes and refused to speak. Her face was tense and blank, as if she was determined to show no expression. Her heart shaped mouth was held tight. Her dark eyes were downcast. Debbie thought she was beautiful and this made Debbie sad. She felt determined to make the child smile. Debbie tried in every way she knew to speak with the girl. She sat down next to her and coaxed gently and patiently, but nothing would open her mouth. When Debbie reached out to touch the child's arm, the little girl fled, crying. Debbie could do nothing but watch her retreat, with a lump in her own throat.

It wasn't until Debbie finally coaxed a happier looking pair of children into a game of Duck Duck Goose that the other kids slowly joined in.

Debbie smiled. *Now it seems like they can just be kids.* She looked at the busy children. *Is this what it's like for Mrs. Levy? I never thought of her as anything but a teacher. But she spends time changing diapers and tucking children into bed at night.*

"Being a Mom must be great. But it's so hard," Debbie said as Leah joined her for a quick breather. "And you've got to do it right. It's so horrible when someone can't do it right." Debbie was thinking of the boy in the corner with his black crayon.

"Yeah," Leah agreed. "My parents sure did a good job with me." She caught Debbie's eye and grinned.

Leah's mother picked the girls up after the event. They climbed in the back seat together. Debbie sat quietly and watched the passing scenery.

"What's on your mind, Deb?"

Debbie told Leah the story of the little girl who ran from her. "I wish I could do something for her. I mean, what difference did today make? Those kids still have all their problems."

"That's you. Out to change the world. Find Esther, whatever. Did you ever stop to think that some things you just can't fix?"

Leah's words stuck in Debbie's head for a long time. When she got home, she went straight to her Club journal:

Some things you just can't fix. That's what Leah said. If I can't, did G-d want it that way? I won't say this to anyone, but maybe we won't find Esther. Maybe some things I just can't fix.

CHAPTER TWENTY-FOUR

Debbie was glad for the distraction of Leah's Bat Mitzvah to keep her mind off Esther. It also helped to avoid thinking about her own twelfth birthday, which was just a few weeks away. She watched her mother methodically working out the details of The Party.

Just as she expected, her parents planned a lovely event for friends and family. They did not need to invite business acquaintances, and that helped to keep the invitation list smaller, and also cut out the need for a lavish affair. Instead, they planned to rearrange their house for the Big Day, clear out the downstairs rooms and stuff a lot of the furniture into the basement. They planned a luncheon at home for friends and family—with pink roses. Mrs. Solomon surprised her with a pink crepe dress to match. Debbie had to admit that the dress was beautiful on her.

Debbie tried on her new dress for Leah. Leah sat on Debbie's bed and kicked off her shoes. Debbie twirled twice. Leah laughed. "See, I told you," Leah said. "Your dress is perfect. And practical, too. Unlike my dress." Leah got a dreamy look on her face. "But it was beautiful, wasn't it?"

Debbie nodded.

"Much too fancy. But I'll love it forever, I think," Leah said. "I'm almost scared to wear it again—it's so beautiful that I'm afraid I'll spill something on it."

Leah's Bat Mitzvah was fun. Since Debbie was practically a sister, she was seated at Leah's table. The two spent a lot of time giggling together, especially when some friends of Leah's parents congratulated Debbie by mistake.

"You'll wear your dress to my party, though, won't you?" Debbie asked.

"And hopefully no one will mix us up!" Debbie felt a wave of relief that Leah wasn't acting distant or jealous because of Rachel.

"It sure is great to have you back, Debs," Leah said.

"Likewise," Debbie said.

While Debbie wasn't looking, spring came. Just as the flowers in the window boxes sprouted new buds, a whole new branch of Debbie's family suddenly appeared. Grandma Eva came again with a glowing report of mail from Lena, her husband, and her two daughters.

"I learned something more," Grandma told Debbie's

family as they sat in the living room together. "They have made lots of phone calls." Grandma Eva turned to smile at Debbie, "They found out some news about Esther."

"What?!" the whole family yelled out eagerly.

"Now don't get your hopes up. It's not so much," she said. "We're not much closer to finding Esther than before. It's just that, since our last conversation, they did speak to someone who knew her in the labor camp."

"That's great! who is it?" Debbie was excited.

"Actually, a famous Russian dissident," Grandma Eva said. "This man got help from the American government and was finally able to leave Russia about fifteen years ago. He's in Israel now. During Lena's search, she realized that this man was imprisoned in the same part of Siberia as Esther. Lena wrote to him quite a few months ago but had not heard back from him. Then," she paused, "she got a letter from him. He said he knew Esther well, and he invited them to call him in Israel."

"So did they?" Debbie asked excitedly.

"Well, of course," Grandma Eva laughed.

"Was he home?" Miri questioned.

"Yes!" Grandma Eva chuckled. "Lena was so excited that neither one of them realized that it was the middle of the night in Israel. They woke him up!"

"And?" Debbie's mother prompted.

"Oh, the things he told them," Grandma Eva sighed. "Life there was hard. But he said that Esther was responsible for keeping up the spirits of so many people. This man said she never lost hope."

Grandma Eva paused, a sad look crossing her face. "This man saw Esther the week before he was released from the camp, which was a couple of years before he was able to leave Russia."

"What? Tell us, what?" Debbie insisted.

"She was there," Grandma Eva answered. "But she was not in great physical shape. The decades of that kind of suffering take their toll."

"But that means we know where Esther was just a few years ago!" Debbie exclaimed. "We can go there and look!"

"Oh, yes, that thought occurred to me, too," Grandma Eva said slowly. "But, Dvorah'leh, he didn't see her, or the person we think is her, just a few years ago. He saw her more than fifteen years ago, and from what this man said about Esther's health, if we went there now, I'm afraid it wouldn't be a successful trip."

After the family recovered from the news, Grandma Eva spoke up again. "It is another lead. Thanks to Debbie we are closer than we ever were. And look at what we're gaining," she reminded the family. "Debbie, come here, child." She gave her granddaughter a hug. "Here's a present for you. It's a letter from Lena's daughter."

Debbie accepted the letter with keen interest. On the cover was written "To Debbie, your cousin Essy." Essy was half a year younger than Debbie. Debbie read the letter. Essy's English was filled with mistakes, perhaps because she'd only been in America for a few years and the family spoke Russian at home. But her message got across. Debbie knew they would become friends. *I'll save this letter and include it in my English project. Maybe we can be pen pals. My project's due in a week! It's a good thing I've already started on my report.* Debbie looked worried.

"Why the long face, little one?" her father asked.

"Oh, I was just thinking about my English project. It's due in a week and I have to get my report done. But Daddy, it's going to look too easy. I mean, all I did was write a few letters."

"You must have had G-d's help," her father replied. His voice sounded husky with emotion, "...and beginner's luck." He winked at her. Somehow, she felt reassured.

Every day of the following week, Debbie got a letter in the mail from Essy. *That girl is quite a writer—another reason why I think I'm going to like her.* She decided to really work at answering her promptly.

Life in Brooklyn sounds so different. The way Essy describes them, the girls there seem older. Essy had shopped in the famous New York City department stores. She rode in a horse-drawn carriage in Central Park for her birthday. She even ate sushi. "But I spat it out when I found out what it was!" Essy wrote. "Ick!! Raw fish!" Debbie laughed.

CHAPTER TWENTY-FIVE

The big day dawned clear and bright. The first small beam of sunlight peeked through the blinds and caught Debbie's dreamy attention. She started to pull the blanket over her head and drift back off to sleep. Suddenly the realization of what day it was went through her mind like a thunderbolt. She leapt out of bed and stood in the middle of her room, her heart pounding. *What do I do first?* The new day beckoned. *But I don't want to rush through this day.*

Debbie put on slippers and padded downstairs. She slipped out the kitchen door and walked out into the back yard. The sweet smell of young grass and damp trees made her sing the word to herself: Spring. She watched as the sky turned a bouquet of pale reds and purples and dusky blues. It was a sunrise of fireworks, a present for her.

Maybe I'm the only girl in the world right now looking at the sky. If G-d creates the world all over again every day for every person, then maybe He made this day beautiful just for me. Because today I start a new part of my Jewish life. It's my Bat Mitzvah birthday present. She stood silently, watching. She took another deep breath of the day and then exhaled.

Debbie shivered. *I wish I'd worn my robe.* She wrapped her arms around herself and started walking quickly back toward the house, then paused at the back door and turned for another look at the day. A voice came from behind her, drawing her out of her reverie: "Happy Bat Mitzvah day! Isn't this a good day for it?"

"Oh, Mom! You startled me. Yes, it is a beautiful day."

Her mother was in the kitchen pulling boxes and containers out of the cupboards and the refrigerator. "What would you like for breakfast? Corn flakes? Fruit and cheese? Whatever you want. Today's your day," her mother said, glancing at the clock, "…as long as you hurry. We've got so much to do before the luncheon!"

"I'd like some waffles, Mom. How about you? I'll make them."

"No, not this time. For once you get to sit and be served. Today's your day." Debbie sat down at the table and poured herself a glass of juice. *Sometimes Mom's neat.* She picked up the pages of her speech from the kitchen table to review them for what seemed to be the billionth time. "Mom, are you sure it's not too long?" she asked after she had turned a few pages. "I don't want to bore all our guests."

"I don't think it's too long," her mother replied. "It may be a little longer than some of your friends' speeches, but it's packed with such interesting Jewish insights. I love the way you apply them to your own life." Her mother looked up from the steaming waffle iron and added, "Of course, I may be biased."

Debbie went on reading. "I could cut out the middle part," she murmured as if she was talking to herself.

"Don't touch a thing," her father said as he came into the room. "I'm not putting on just any old fancy luncheon. This fancy luncheon's going to be full of food for thought. And your speech is perfect."

"Okay, I'm convinced," Debbie said, smiling at her Dad. "Thanks."

The rest of the morning was full of the tumult of their preparations. The telephone rang endlessly. Debbie paced back and forth and rehearsed her speech—endlessly. There was the flurry of bathing and dressing. Debbie's mother was busy directing the two young women who were the caterers.

In the middle of it all, Debbie retreated to her room and drew her chair up to her bedroom window. She held the book of Psalms that Mrs. Levy gave her as an early Bat Mitzvah present.

Mrs. Levy said different Psalms are said for different

occasions. Today I'm finishing twelve years of my life. I'm starting my thirteenth year!

She turned to Psalm 13, the year she was now beginning. She read through the lines. She liked the end.

"I trust in Your loving kindness,
my heart will exult in Your deliverance.
I will sing to G-d
for He has dealt kindly with me."

Debbie thought of everything she'd been through since her last birthday: the search for Esther, finding new family, her success in swimming, the new worlds that opened up to her because of the Bat Mitzvah Club.

There's so much to thank G-d for. I know everything's not perfect. Esther's still missing, and who knows what horrible things might have happened to her.

She pictured the troubled faces of the children at the Home. But somehow, she felt lucky. "G-d has dealt kindly with me." *That's a good line. Thanks, G-d. I'm going to try to do what You want."*

CHAPTER TWENTY-SIX

Debbie gasped. The house was just as she imagined. She felt she was visiting a new place. Downstairs they had a large, open area from the entryway through the large family room on the right and the dining room on the left. Now it was completely transformed. Round, elegantly arranged tables filled the entire area, covered with rose colored tablecloths and napkins that set off the creamy white china and glistening silver. Fresh pink rosebuds were mirrored in the shimmering goblets. Cloth-lined baskets held crusty rolls. Debbie wandered through as if she was in a fairyland.

Miri followed with her camera, ready to snap pictures for the family. *Mommy must have given her that job. Good—it'll keep her busy. I just hope she manages to take some good pictures.* Earlier in the week, Debbie, Miri, and

Leah had assembled one hundred pink-and-white-striped gift bags. Now one sat next to each place. Each gift bag held a small prayer book inscribed with Debbie's name and Bat Mitzvah date, some small foil-wrapped chocolates, and a delicate mirror set into a gold frame.

"Mom, it's gorgeous!" Debbie whispered. She touched Miri's arm. "Miri, take a picture!" Miri obediently snapped the scene. Debbie sighed, worried. "You better take two or three shots, OK?"

Debbie began to feel weak with nervousness. She took a chair off to the side. *Ohhh, I wish I didn't have to speak. I'm going to forget how to read. I'll stand there and stumble over my words and feel sooo dumb.*

Mrs. Levy walked in. She greeted Debbie's parents and then went over to Debbie, who was chewing a fingernail and staring at her speech. "I'll bet you've worked so hard on that speech you could recite it in your sleep!" Mrs. Levy said sympathetically.

Debbie nodded.

Mrs. Levy pulled up a chair. "Debbie, I'd like for us to have a private minute before all of your guests arrive. Can you concentrate now?"

Debbie nodded again. "I think so."

Mrs. Levy reached into her handbag and took out a candle and a small glass candleholder. It was small, but pretty. Debbie looked at the swirls of color in the glass. *Nice.* "I know I've already given you a Bat Mitzvah gift but, well, this is in honor of your mitzvot."

"Thanks," Debbie said, and accepted the offered gift.

"This is one of the three special mitzvot for Jewish women."

She remembered the Club meeting when Mrs. Levy spoke about those three mitzvot. She tried to imagine herself raising a Jewish family. *Maybe Mom and I can start baking challah so we can separate a piece of the dough and say the blessing.*

Mrs. Levy touched her hand. "Debbie... I think you're special. You have an unusual ability to help others—and yourself." Debbie looked at her thoughtfully. She wasn't sure. *Myself?*

Mrs. Levy didn't answer. Instead she leaned forward and touched Debbie's arm. "Debbie, I want you to make sure that your Jewish soul always shines in you. Your mitzvot will make sure of that. Your Shabbat candles will remind you." Debbie returned the intent look in Mrs. Levy's eyes. She felt right then that Mrs. Levy really cared about her. She felt deeply connected to her teacher at that moment, as if she was recognizing something that she had not realized before. *She makes me feel so... Jewish.*

A soul shines in a person like a candle. "Mrs. Levy," she said. "Is everyone a candle?"

"I think so. I think a lot of people aren't aware of it, and I think you are aware. That gives you a special responsibility."

"What is it?"

"To know and use all of your fine abilities. I think you found out that when you give of yourself for a mitzvah, you don't lose. You gain. And the fire in you kindles a fire in others. I know you can understand what I'm saying because of the way you managed your search for Esther, and the way your dedication got other people involved."

Debbie smiled with pride.

"I hope your candle will burn a bright path for you. Always."

"Thanks, Mrs. Levy. Thanks so much." *It will. I promise.*

Debbie looked up and felt faint. While she was huddling with Mrs. Levy, the house suddenly filled up. School friends, Bat Mitzvah Club members, relatives, and family friends chatted with one another. With all the tables filled, it seemed like much more than the one hundred places that they set. Leah caught Debbie's eye and waved. "Gorgeous!" she mouthed across the crowd.

Debbie's mother came over and pulled Debbie to her feet. "Come on, daughter mine." Her face was flushed with excitement. "Curtain's up!"

CHAPTER TWENTY-SEVEN

Debbie and her mother walked slowly through the crowd holding hands. She felt somewhat shy and was glad to have her mother with her. Her mother looked beautiful and so confident—like a shield and also a guide for Debbie. Everywhere they were stopped for good wishes, greetings and congratulations. After what seemed like forever to Debbie, they finally slipped into their seats at their table at the front. Debbie's father stood up to speak.

Mr. Solomon's new, black suit made him seem more commanding. *He bought it especially for my Bat Mitzvah.* She liked the way he looked in it. A new yarmulka was perched on the top of his head. His brown hair was newly trimmed, which made the place on top of his head where his hair was thinning more obvious, but she liked that. The few streaks of gray were recent arrivals. So were the new lines she noticed in his forehead.

First her father thanked everyone for coming. Then he continued.

"Akiba was a poor shepherd who grew up with no education. He worked for a very wealthy man. The man was called Kalba Savua, and he had an only child, a daughter named Rachel, on whom he lavished his wealth." Mr. Solomon paused and looked at both of his daughters seated nearby. "I have two daughters, so I doubly sympathize." Everyone laughed.

"Kalba Savua sought only the finest suitors for his daughter, who had grown to be a gentle and wise young woman. Sadly, she rejected one young man after the next.

"Rachel had been watching Akiba for quite some time. She had an unusual insight, and she recognized greatness in him. Eventually, against her father's will, she married him. Her father was deeply hurt and disowned his daughter. Akiba and Rachel lived in poverty.

"Rachel urged Akiba to get an education, but Akiba resisted. 'My head is like a rock,' he said. 'How can I begin to learn like a child at this point in my life? It will not go in.' The idea was foreign to him, but Rachel persisted."

Again, Mr. Solomon paused, shuffled his papers, and cleared his throat. Debbie saw the lump move up and down on his throat that told her he was about to say something that was difficult for him. "Again, I... sympathize. I am pleased and proud that we decided to put our girls in a Jewish school, but at the time, I felt like Akiba did. I did not think it was possible that anything could lead to my own Jewish learning. Like Rachel, my girls have inspired me.

"One day, Akiba brought his sheep to a stream to drink. There, in the stream, was a ledge that formed a pool, and beneath it, a large rock. The water of the pool dripped slowly down. The falling drops of water had carved a hole in the ancient rock. When he saw that, he knew that the words of Torah, one drop at a time, would penetrate his forty-year-old head. This was Akiba's greatness—that he could look at the scene and see G-d's message to him in it. With sacrifice for both of them, and to Rachel's joy, he went to learn—and became a great leader and teacher, a guide for our people through difficult times.

"Now, why am I telling you this story? Because I was thinking about Debbie's perseverance in the project she undertook, which you will soon hear about, and this is the thought that occurred to me.

"Let's say the hole was just completed as Akiba walked up. Now, what if just one of the millions of drops of water that formed that rock had said, 'What am I? One drop? I don't count. It doesn't matter. I'm turning back. I don't make a difference, anyway.' What would we have? No hole in a rock. No Rabbi Akiba.

"I know I feel like that at times. What am I? A drop in the sea of humanity? What's one little mitzvah, or one single unfulfilled effort? The story of Rabbi Akiba says each drop is really momentous, and so is each effort, no matter how small, that we make.

"Debbie apparently understood this better than I did. She undertook a project that we gave up on long ago, and she seemed to know that every inch of effort made a difference. She knew better than we did. And she was right." He looked over at his daughter and their eyes met. She felt he was telling her something. She felt a wave of gratitude.

"Here's Debbie."

Debbie took a deep breath. Her hands were shaking with nervousness. She looked at her mother, who squeezed her hand, smiling encouragement, and stood up. Slowly, Debbie looked over the crowd. Here were her parents and Miri, and her parents' friends. Here were Erica, Sarah, Michelle, Jennifer, Amy, and the rest of her friends from school, swimming and the Bat Mitzvah Club. Here was Grandma Eva. Debbie felt a surge of warmth for her grandmother. She wanted to step down right there and fall into her grandmother's arms. She swallowed. Here was Leah, her very best friend—sitting right next to Rachel! Even Mr. Hankins was here. And sitting quietly on the side was Mrs. Levy with her husband. *All these people are here just for me. We have all these wonderful friends*! For a moment she stood still and listened to the clink of water glasses and the lingering, hushed talk. She thought of Mrs. Levy, who did not have to ask for quiet, and waited patiently. Soon, all eyes were on Debbie. She arranged her papers in her hands, took another deep, shaky breath, and began.

"I'd like to dedicate my speech to Esther," she began. "That's my great-aunt Esther. I haven't been the same since I first heard about Esther a few months ago. My family knows that—and I apologize if I was a little hard to live with." There was a scattering of laughter. Debbie's voice slowly gained strength.

"Esther was... is... well, we're still not sure... my grand-mother's sister. I didn't know she existed until a few months ago. She left her family as a young woman to help the resistance in Europe before World War II. She was willing to risk everything to save Jewish lives. Her family never saw her again."

Again, there was murmuring. Again, she waited, listening to her heart pound.

"After the war, they tried everything to find her, but they never could. Miri and I never knew about her; maybe they didn't want to worry us. When my Bat Mitzvah was coming, my family decided to tell me. I hope they're not sorry they did." Her family laughed.

Some people were straining to get a view of her family. Suddenly the picture of her family all together in front of her, laughing together, warmed her. *They're all here for me*. She felt more confident.

"Today, some of the lists that different places use to search for people are on computers. The Holocaust Museum Research Department has them. They gave us a few names. We wrote and called, and it looks like we found Esther's family!" Debbie paused and drew in her breath.

She looked up for a minute at the crowd. *It's OK to look. Go ahead. You can do it.* She thought of Mrs. Brown. *This is like swimming—just dive in and don't think about anything but the job.* Seeing all the faces wasn't making her so nervous any more. She continued to read.

"I'm glad we did it. I found out about doing something when you don't even know how to start, but you know you have to figure out how. My parents say this is what happens when you don't give up, no matter what.

"None of this would have meant so much to me if it weren't for Mrs. Levy and the Bat Mitzvah Club. That's where I learned the importance of our roots in the Torah. And that's where I learned about my Jewish soul. I always felt that my Jewish soul made me keep on looking.

"Now, I'm supposed to say something from the Torah." There were a few titters. She looked back down at her paper.

"My birthday is near Passover. Passover is about how the Jewish people escaped being slaves to the Egyptians and how they began their journey to Israel. But Mrs. Levy said Passover is about freeing ourselves from our limitations and going above all of the things that keep us from being everything we can be. When she said that, it sounded just like Mrs. Brown, my swimming coach." She looked up again, at all the faces, all of them looking at her. The next part of her speech was embarrassing. *Go. Just keep on going. Don't think.*

"Really, most of the time I just think I can't do more. Or I think I'm weaker than I am and let myself be pulled to do something just because other girls are doing it and I don't want to be left out. But Passover says our mind can tell us the right thing to do—to follow what the Torah teaches. It says we can be stronger than the desires we might have. When we are free to think and we are not ruled by our hearts, we are really free."

Debbie felt grateful to her mother for helping her with this part of her speech. I knew what I wanted to say, but only Mom had the right words.

Debbie looked at her family. A few of the people in the room nodded their heads, waiting for her to continue. She realized how long she had paused.

"I just have a few more things to say before you get to the food," Debbie said with a smile. "My great-aunt Esther has the same name as Queen Esther who worked to save the Jewish people even though it was very dangerous for her.

"Devorah was a judge. She was in charge of the army and because of her the Jewish people won major battles. Most of all, though, G-d gave Devorah the ability to help other people."

Debbie gazed out at her guests. "So... now I want to go by my Jewish name. Then, every time I hear my name—Devorah—it will remind me of the abilities G-d has given me."

She stood tall, and her voice became softer. "We did not find my Aunt Esther," she said. "I suppose it's possible that we won't find her at all. I understand now that that's in

G-d's hands. But I learned alot from her. I hope I can be like Esther every day and always use my Jewish soul to make the world a better place."

The hush that filled the room was suddenly broken by applause. The clapping intensified as, a few at a time, Debbie's guests rose from their seats. All at once, Debbie's parents and Leah stood up, too.

Debbie could do nothing but stand there in shock as she watched more and more of the guests stand until all of the tables were surrounded with standing, clapping, cheering people. Debbie's face went white and then red. At first she felt very embarrassed, and her knees felt weak. *No! I won't be afraid. This is good.* Then she felt relief and a wave of pride wash over her. She lifted her chin and stood tall. The guests slowly stopped clapping and took their seats again as Debbie's mother made her way to Debbie's side.

"Thank you, Devorah," her mother said in an emotion filled voice. "I've never felt so proud." She turned toward the guests. "I'd like to introduce some very special guests. They traveled a good distance in order to be here with us today. You see, our family has never been quite complete—until now. We want to welcome our long-lost family, the children and grandchildren of Devorah's Esther!"

Everyone cheered. Debbie was completely surprised. *What? What?!!*

Walking toward Debbie was a girl who looked just like the old pictures of Esther that she had tacked to the bulletin board in her room.

The girl stood before her and offered her hand. "Mazel tov, Devorah!" she said in an accented voice.

When Debbie saw how much the girl looked like the young Esther, she was momentarily confused.

But... but Esther can't still look so young...

The girl grinned. "Surprise! I'm your cousin, Essy!"

An enormous smile spread on Debbie's face at the incredible resemblance. *Yes! Now I really know it's her!* She threw her arms around Essy. She felt the closing of a gap that had been open for a long time.

"This is the best Bat Mitzvah present in the whole world!" Debbie told her. Then she looked at her newfound cousin. Her cousin held her at arm's length and beamed. Debbie extended her hand in friendship. "Essy, welcome to the family!" Essy grabbed her hand and shook it vigorously. "Thanks," she said. "Oh, thank you. I am so very glad to be here!"